LIVING WITHOUT SHADOWS

Living Without Shadows

This is a work of fiction. Names, characters, businesses, places, events, locals, and incidents are either the products of the authors imagination or used in a fictitious manner. Any resemblance to actual persons, living or dead, or actual events is purely coincidental.

The opinions expressed in this manuscript are solely the opinions of the author and do not represent the opinions of the author and do not represent the opinions or thoughts of the publisher. The author has represented and warranted full ownership and/or legal right to publish all the materials in this book.

Outskirts Press, Inc.

http://www.outskirtspress.com

ISBN:978-1-9772-5879-3

PRINTED IN THE UNITED OF AMERICA

With grateful thanks to:

John McComb

Karen Kaufman

Marcelle Berenson

Miriam Mabalane

Rachel Mendez

Norman & Lena Woolf

Nicole Ohliger

Rhona (Naturman) Mathews

BOOK I

Chapter 1

Too Little and Too Much

SHE woke in the morning, drowsy and numb from the sleeping pills she'd taken the previous night. The heavy curtains, still drawn, blocked the bright sunlight that would have otherwise focused the details of the bedroom in sharp contrast.

Her husband had already woken, shaved, dressed, eaten and left the house by 7 o'clock. Somehow she had slept through that daily ritual, as she had done for years.

It hadn't always been that way, but now she couldn't remember when the change happened.

She might have blamed her state on the sleeping pills, but then she knew she took at least some of the pills to make his looming presence and insistent desire merge with her veil of semi-awareness, until lifted, it let her through to the other side, and safety.

Often, even without his presence, there was a point at which she couldn't bear the speed and intensity of her thoughts, the oppression of her loneliness.

Lying in bed awake in the unbroken night, silent except for the occasional snore from the body next to her, echoed occasionally by a siren, far off and muffled by the heavy curtains.

For her, there was no miracle jump, no natural volition, no synthesis of events, no conscious decision to move from one desired experience to another desired experience. She had to endure time. She endured that in-between, the undesired, the unknown, the unexpected, the unhappiness. As time passed, the significant singular events or objects reflected less and less importance in the perspective of her subservience to the whole.

Sometimes she couldn't recognize herself anymore. She looked at her reflection in the mirrors of the wardrobe as she passed. The reflection showed someone else, recognizable and familiar, but someone else, damaged, worn, overweight, spotted, transparent, scarred, scared.

Her awareness of the gradual development and eventual impermanence of her notion of Self, often depleted, renewed only for precarious moments.

There were days when she wondered why she felt nothing had changed at all, just a few moments, or perhaps an hour, or perhaps a day ago.

There were moments it seemed as if she were in a cave with only her echo to talk with. It was the only satisfactory way to survive all those years, at least until she was naked in the cold water of the bathtub, unable to extricate herself, watching her skin wrinkle as her alternating sobs and silent screams found neither respite nor response.

There were many details she didn't remember, and many details she remembered too much.

...~...

Chapter 2

The Bell (1)

S

SHE sighed. The three children had gone to school. She didn't know that for a fact, she presumed it.

She also presumed Lilian, the head maid, had taken care of their breakfast, washed their clothes and placed them ironed and starched in the various drawers of their cupboards ready for the next morning.

When she got out of bed and left the bedroom, two or three hours later, she wouldn't confirm if the children were absent then either. Instead, the silence, the isolation of the distant sounds of the maids going about their work would confirm her suspicion until the children returned around 2:00 p.m. when she did not need to speculate on their absence any longer. They were no longer absent.

In the darkness, she reached for the switch of the domed crystal lamp next to her bed.

The faceted, reflected, and refracted light cast by rainbow slivers around the room illuminated the six pills she had placed in the small pink ashtray with the gold edge and her glass of water.

One at a time, she swallowed the pills, so familiar with them by now she didn't expect their effects with any inquisitiveness or anticipation, but with the resignation which is sometimes formed by habit.

Prescriptions for these drugs were no problem for her. The local doctor wrote prescriptions for the ladies of the neighborhood for whatever drug they had decided was in vogue.

Each day they called each other, eight, nine, ten calls in a row. After the usual enquiries about the children and before the arrangements to play tennis or their next 'Dinner and a Show' with their husbands, they would discuss the pills. The effects and the side effects, the durations and the palpitations, the pitfalls and the falling-overs, the alternatives and the combinations.

Each day, they reported to each other and then made their mental notes to call the local doctor and get the changes or additions made to their prescriptions.

The delivery of the prescriptions by the balding pharmacists, the very tall and very large balding pharmacist, married to the woman that her husband was attracted to, and later, replaced by the tiny and very thin, bald pharmacist.

She felt the coolness of the water flow down her throat and into her stomach, but she ignored the uniqueness of that sensation. Instead, it was a reminder of her primary concern, her growing hunger.

With difficulty and with a sigh, not that much different from her earlier sigh, but edging closer towards a grunt or a groan, she moved the weight of her body and reached over to press the electric bell on the wall next to her bed.

One ring called Lilian, two rings called the second maid, three rings brought the garden boy.

The same series of rings contributed to the same results when she used the bell under the carpet in the dining room, when she had guests over for dinner, which, except for the annual family get-togethers, twice a year, on the Holy Days, didn't happen anymore.

In the room known as the Breakfast Room, which hosted all the family meals and not breakfast, the bell was not as complex as that in the dining room.

The Breakfast Room bell was a small silver handbell with a rounded and well-worn black wooden handle that revealed the bare wood beneath parts of its painted surface.

This bell's mechanical complexity required the dexterity of the hand to have it ring singularly, one, two, or three times, to summon a particular servant. It was almost impossible to have the bell ring, one, two, or three strikes, even for someone with youthful dexterity, unlike the arthritic motions of the Madam's hand. The bell always echoed with multiple strikes of lesser and lesser volume as the volition of the striker lost momentum, or until it was muffled by contact with the tablecloth.

An alternative method of ringing might have been to ring with a burst of fading strikes, in a series of one, two, or three bursts. One burst of strikes for Lilian, two bursts for the second maid, and three bursts for the garden boy.

But that would have meant some exertion, and besides, it would have violated the silence at the table.

It had been, and would often be, days, and occasionally weeks of silence.

...❧...

Chapter 3

The Silence

THIS was not the silence of one hand clapping. This was not the silence of dignity, or of Divine Light, or of consideration, or empathy.

This was not the silence of hope or prayer, the silence of fantasy or desire, the silence of growth, the silence of social amnesia.

This was the silence of vengeance, the silence of repose before striking.

This was the silence of fear of that moment of eruption when the Master would rear on his hind legs, frothing at the mouth, stuttering with spittle, demanding ownership of his piece of pie.

This was silence as a weapon, with no given opportunity for dialogue that may reveal some opening to the soft belly, where there might be rotten and forgotten acquiescences to the notions of frailty or kindness or understanding or compromise.

This was the silence of his self-ordained power, his regal frustration with his own ability to form any view or perspective of the consequences of his actions on others, or the reality of his enjoyment in causing the cowering of others, of his own victimization, of the emotional baggage he bore from his father, and his father before him, and his father's father before him, and which he imposed on his children.

For weeks at a time, the family sat at dinner in a silence stretched taut by the turnbuckle of repressed violence torqued to its maximum, during which the Master would demand various food items or refuse others from behind the evening newspaper.

This was a silence which reduced the others in the family to the kaleidoscope of their witness, faceted and fractured reflections of their lack of understanding and inability to accept each other from within that lens.

This was the silence of heated argument throttled by a toxic flood rising in the throat of kindness, the silence of the unfettered recognition of the commonality of their experience, of their ultimate defeat, and of their survival.

This was the silence of the unacknowledged Other.

...❧...

Chapter 4

Baiting the Children

THE Madam's children, Rebecca, the eldest, Nathan, and Shaye the youngest, were desperate to hold up some sense of one-dimensional truth, some single unchanging monolith of continuity, something they could identify as the Truth, something they could grasp onto as Reality. It always evaded them. The moving target of the Master's narcissist and misogynist personality evaded all capture.

Something could always coerce the Madam to go down the pathway of intention to discover her ulterior motives. The path was sometimes a lengthy one once identified, but even though fraught with frustration, usually the process was quite conclusive and her intimate and layered intentions became quite clear. Constantly critical of others, she was ultimately self-critical to the point of self-abuse and eventually self-defeat.

The Master, by contrast, possessed the unenviable quality of viciousness in combination with a certain perverse enjoyment in the attack's process.

He invented arguments. He made statements of 'fact'. He implied knowledge, or experience. He faked commitment or dedication to ideals. Being the opportunist he was, at any unexpected moment, he laid the trap. He dangled the bait, infused the air with the acrid pungency of deceit and allure. With calculated attention, he set the lures of politics, or jealousy, whereby he could attract and with brutal incisiveness eliminate, belittle or dismiss the children's responses to his snare. He waited in the shadow of refute to pounce on some supposed inconsistency, some supposed falsehood in the children's reply, so that he could lop the head off the beast, grind the notion into the dust with his heel, piss on the corpse as he stood above it with a sardonic smile, while he incised the concepts of those frail children trying vainly to pierce the surface of the suffocating envelope of their imbibed sense of nihilist self-worth, coerced, inherited, accepted and integrated into their being, to where there was no longer any distinction between the annihilating intentions of their father and their own debilitating self-destruction.

...❧...

Chapter 5

The Bell (2)

SOMETIMES the Madam lost patience, and in a quick gesture put the bell down on the table, muffling the striker. She ignored the number of rings the striker made. In between her fleeting glances at the food on the plates of the others at the table, she would spend a large part of the subsequent meal staring at the bell, pondering her failure.

The mist never retreated.

A single shaking of the bell, resulting in a ringing of whatever duration, sufficed for the silver bell with the black wooden handle in the breakfast room. This ring summoned Lilian, who, if was not needed to do a task or have a consultation, was told to call one of the other servants or to communicate a message to them.

At times, the Madam pressed what was supposed to be the bell button next to her bed, but instead of the comfortingly familiar buzz, the emergency siren wailed forth, occasionally combining with others in the neighborhood, like the sirens of several boats caught in fog. Only there was no fog, the howl was insistently constant and without the lilting fading in and out as the strong wind pushes the sound to and fro.

…❧…

Chapter 6

The Living Room

THE electric bell under the sculpted burgundy red carpet with the white fringe in the dining room had seemed a unique and luxurious feature when they had bought the house.

At the beginning, she had often made a detour in her visitor's tour to point out the bell, but the bell had become redundant, to the point of annoyance.

There were many redundant features, not all of them were annoying, some sad monuments to various dreams, desires or demons.

The shape of one side of the mid-century rancher house was a rounded ship's prow, complete with concrete portholes. It overlooked the swimming pool and the various neighbors' yards and the small lake with the willows down the road.

It was a redundant feature compared to the distinctive and sophisticated impression it had initially served when they purchased the house.

'The Living Room' was redundant, just like 'The Bar', and 'The Rumpus Room'. Just like 'The Bidet' and 'The Changing Rooms', 'The Iron Gate' and 'The Breakfast Nook'. Just like 'The Bell' under the carpet in 'The Dining Room'.

'The Living Room', like many other redundancies, held its secrets. Each redundancy had features or had held purposes that one member of the family or the other kept to themselves. They shared none of these secrets with each other.

These secrets were very different to the secrets they did share, many years later, like the round bedroom window at night with the palm tree shadow that was so mysterious and foreboding, or how the Master had his young son's piss in the mouth of Rebecca while she slept, and he watched.

Use of the living room was used for only one occasion other than as a moribund display. Otherwise it went untouched besides for the labors of the maids and the garden boy.

Once a week, the garden boy polished the wooden parquet floor to a mirror finish while the maids dusted, wiped, or polished the various pieces of furniture, the paintings and the hand-blown glass ornaments from Venice.

Once a week the living room was alive. Lilian or the garden boy tuned the Master's radio to 'Their' radio station, and the music blared out at maximum volume.

Their culture, over the centuries, had developed a rhythmic structure to their music that was both hypnotic, energetic, transforming, and transporting.

Depending on the context, the music could elevate or console, pacify or cajole.

This was Africa, where lions ate their offspring in unfettered acts of fratricide. Where competing lionesses, who not long before competed for the attention of the lion, would join in common defense of their offspring from him.

This was Africa, where the heat of the road burned feet so they scarred into impervious pads of callous that allowed young boys to run in the long grass, over sharp stones, to climb trees without ropes, to dance for hours, first lifting their legs until their uplifted knees struck the pad of their open palm held across their forehead, and then bringing the foot down, pounding into the hard earth which lifted in a puff of red dust.

Africa.

…❧…

Chapter 7

Black and White Buttons

OFTEN, a man, sometimes two men, walked down a suburban road, sometimes hand in hand, or sometimes, one with a guitar and the other with a small piano accordion or a squash box.

The beaten and worn guitar had no more than two or three strings, often made of fencing wire, while the squash box often had small insets of faux mother-of-pearl at the handles, worn away to white at all the points where the players fingers touched the combinations of black buttons that drew the varied sounds from the instrument.

Walking down the street, large carved wooden discs in their ear lobes almost reaching their shoulders, the guitar player played the same two chords, over and over, repeatedly, while the squash box player played two other chords, over and over again, repeatedly, mile after mile, never missing a beat or varying the chord or the sequence of the chord to where there was no beginning or middle or end. To where there never had been a beginning. To where there would never be an end. To where the instrument no longer mattered, guitar or voice, drum or accordion.

There was only that walk from one suburb to the other. There was only that trench to dig, spade by spade, their voices in unison. There was only that load to carry, or that gold to pick out of the wall of the mine, one-mile deep underground. Again, and again, over and over, again and again, over and over.

Again and again, over and over, again and again, over and over, the tune flowed, blaring out of the transistor radio, rattling the key in its lock, in sync, in counterpoint to the guitar, the saxophone, the accordion, the drums. The same tune, again and again, over and over, again and again, over and over.

The Manservant on his knees polishing the large floor, by hand, with a coarse bristle brush, his swirling hands moving across the floor, replicating, weaving with the rhythm of the music while the Maids' swayed and dusted, swayed and dusted, stepping in rhythm from one article to another, from one ornament to the next, from one painting to the other, across the room until the entire room reflected the bright sunlight streaming through the transparent picture window which threw rippled reflections from the swimming pool onto the ceiling where fashionable concealed fluorescent lights cowered behind the white stucco facade.

There were only rare moments when magic permeated this house, but polishing the floors and dusting the furniture in "The Living Room" once a week was one of them.

Most of the family never saw or experienced this moment, which didn't last many years.

They aren't home.

Or.

They have sequestered themselves in the bedroom with the curtains drawn.

And.

After some years, the Master replaced the white Bakelite tube radio with a transistor version that required a key to power it on and off. He had purchased the radio for his son on his thirteenth birthday, but with time, he had appropriated it for himself to listen to the news or to listen in privacy to Frank

Sinatra or Nat King Cole.

On one occasion, the Master returned home after work, turned on the radio expecting to hear Frank or Nat, but the blaring rhythms of 'Their' music greeted him instead. The servants had forgotten to return the dial to its original location and volume, hiding their use of the radio that day.

The Master was furious. From that day on he took the key from the radio and hid it in his 'secret location'.

Thus ended the magical moments in 'The Living Room'.

Or rather, so he thought.

Not that he wanted to end the magical moments in 'The Living Room'. He didn't even know that those moments happened. He just didn't want 'Them' listening to 'Their' music on His radio. Or He just didn't want 'Them' listening to 'Their' music on His radio and using up His batteries!

It was a situation not unlike 'The Disappearance of the Sugar'.

...~...

Chapter 8

A Head Maids Secret

THE Madam always bought two types of meat when she went to the butcher. She still bought two types of meat later when she had the meat delivered by a family friend rather than going to the butcher and standing in line with the sawdust on the floor and the smell of biltong in the air.

She bought regular meat for the family, and 'Boys' Meat' for the servants, both male and female.

'Boys Meat' was meat of unknown origin. It could be horse meat, or the off-cuts from pigs, cows or goats. It could be the rear or the front of the animal, but was definitely not kosher.

Lilian, in charge of cooking, substituted the 'Boys' Meat' for the New York Strip steaks or the Pot Roasts, which the Madam had bought for the family.

Lilian, together with the other servants, enjoyed the delicacies of T-Bone and Rump steak in the bright fuchsia laundry room blackened by the paraffin stove, while the family chewed unknowingly on the 'Boys' Meat' in the Breakfast Room.

…❧…

THE Master's Secret: He had married the Madam for her family's money.

Another Lilian Secret: She knew where the Master hid the key for the radio.

Rebecca's Secret: Telling no one, she took a chocolate from the drawer next to the Masters' bed.

Nathan's Secret: Telling no one, he took a chocolate from the drawer next to the Masters' bed.

Shaye's Secret: Telling no one, he took a chocolate from the drawer next to the Masters' bed.

Another Master's Secret: He knew the children were taking his chocolate from the drawer next to his bed.

Another Lilian Secret: The Government said it was illegal for the servants to have liquor, so they made their own as they had done for centuries and sold it secretly out of the backyards of the Madam's houses, supplementing their incomes and weaving an intricate web of connections between houses and neighborhoods.

Lilian ran an illegal liquor outlet from the backyard of the Madams house for many years, until the Government with a rare gesture to the equality of the races, made alcohol legal for all races.

Lilian still took small amounts from the Master's supply of whiskey and brandy, replacing the missing volume with dark brewed tea. She was quite aware of the pen hash marks the Master had drawn on the label of the bottle to document the volume of the liquor within.

…❧…

ANOTHER Master's Secret.

He replaced the whiskey in the Glenlivet bottle with cheap whiskey and then reveled in the compliments he received from his guests as to the quality and flavor of the Glenlivet whiskey.

It wasn't clear whether the Master reveled in his ability to deceive his guests or whether he gleaned a sense of superiority from knowing that his guests were fooling themselves. Or perhaps both. They were fooled, and he had fooled them.

The guests didn't know the Masters' secret.

Neither the Guests nor the Master knew the Maids' secret of replacing the whiskey with tea.

…❧…

ANOTHER Master's Secret.

The only other activity in the Living Room, besides the weekly cleaning by the Servants, was when Rebecca's dates arrived to pick her up.

The Master would answer the front door and invite the young man into the Living Room.

"Have a seat."

"Would you like a drink?"

"Would you like a cigarette?"

A positive answer to either of these questions would disqualify the young man immediately from dating Rebecca.

But no young man ever replied in the affirmative, even though several of her suitors smoked or drank or partook of both. Rebecca knew the Masters' secret and had forewarned her suitors of this examination by her father..

The young man, Barry, who became her husband, forewarned like the others, did not need to be as he partook in neither of the two vices.

Barry's vice was different. His vice was to accumulate money.

Impressed by the furniture and the velvet embossed wallpaper in the Living Room with the concealed fluorescent lighting, Barry was more impressed with the velvet embossed wallpaper than the furniture or the lighting.

Barry was in the big city now, several hundred miles from his hometown, a small rural community where his father made a living selling second-hand cars.

Barry didn't let on until years later that the imagined fortune held by this family of his future wife didn't exist. That however didn't stop him from attempting to draw as much money as he could from them in upcoming years.

The living room was unlike anything he had ever seen.

The tassels that hang from the silk curtains.

The rococo style furniture designed by the Madam's father in his furniture factory, made in three styles that appeared in the factory catalogue. Under each style, a disguised but brilliant use of the names of each of his three children; The 'Esti', a large sofa, The Baylah, a smaller sofa, and The Lisli, a matching chair.

The shiny chevron parquet floor with its reflection of the soft light of concealed fluorescent bulbs.

The large Venetian blown glass ornaments of clowns, donkeys, ballet dancers, and a seal balancing a ball on its nose.

The genuine hand painted oil paintings of scenes of foreign vegetable and flower markets, sunsets on distant harbors, and in a corner, a portrait of a clown with a tear in his eye.

And through the glass doors, the bump of the bell under the burgundy carpet in the adjoining dining room.

...❧...

Chapter 9

Farfi

THE Madam always had difficulty finding the bell under the carpet with her foot without bending to the side to peer under the table, searching for the telltale bump that would define its location.

Firstly, if she located the bump in the darkness under the table, not only could she not coordinate her visual memory of where the bump was located with the tactile feel for it with her foot, but her feet were too short to apply the required pressure at the required angle without sliding halfway off her chair.

Secondly, the bell caused a disturbance.

Sometimes, while savoring her food, she would inadvertently press the bell with her foot. Thereupon, Lilian, somewhat dismayed at the length and insistence of the ringing bell, would enter asking, “What is it, Madam?”

Although this sometimes served as a somewhat humorous interlude in the meager conversation of the evening, it was embarrassing having the spotlight of attention placed on her by her inadvertent call.

Between bunions and chilblains on her toes, flat feet and dropped arches, cracked and dried out foot-soles from carrying her weight, and the embarrassment in front of her guests, she abandoned the electric bell in the Dining Room floor and replaced it with a hand-held china bell in the shape of a little blonde girl with bright red lips wearing a white ball gown.

…⁂…

SHE rang the bell next to the bed once to call Lilian.

Now she had to wait for the servant's response, hoping against hope that it wasn't the second or fourth Thursday of the month.

The second or the Fourth Thursday of the month were the days that Lilian had to herself and known as the 'Girl's Day Off.'

The Maids were "Girls" no matter what age they were.

The Male servants were 'Boys' no matter what age they were.

'Boys' Meat' was meat for the servants, both male and female.

"Kaffir" was the derogatory term used to refer to any black person, maid or garden boy, female or male, child or adult.

'Kaffir' was drawn from Arabic roots meaning 'irreligious person' or 'infidel'. The reference ignored whether the black person referred to was Episcopalian, Catholic, Jesuit, Baptist or one of several religious sects or practices that the servants took part in, sometimes in combination and sometimes alternately.

Some servants believed emphatically in theories of dreams and chance as well as the more formalized religions like Shamanism or Christianity.

…⁂…

IN the sphere of dreams and chance, the Chinaman was the conveyor of all things in the matter of 'Farfi'.

'Farfi' was a system whereby servants picked numbers according to their dreams or intuitions and then placed bets with the Chinaman. The Chinaman paid out winning numbers, each of which had different odds. It was an informal backyard illegal lottery with all the resulting secrecy, intrigue and mystique.

Each week, the servants intently discussed the numbers amongst themselves, making their bets and waiting through the day, usually a Friday, for the results.

Any of the servants could tell you the characteristics and odds of the thirty-six Farfi numbers without a second thought. Just as they could fluently change their language from their home language to any of the eleven languages most could speak; Ndebele, Xhosa, Zulu, Pedi, Sotho, Tswana, Swati, Venda, Tsonga, English or Afrikaans.

Each number, 1 through 36, had a particular character or description:

1 King

2 Monkey

3 Sea water

4 A Dead Man or Woman

5 Tiger

6 A New Cow

7 Crime

8 A Pig

9 A Moon

10 Eggs

11 A Carriage

12 Dead Woman or a Dead Man

13 A Big Fish or a Small Fish

14 Magogo - old Woman

15 Scabarige - a rubber neck (loose woman)

16 Majuba - Birds

17 Diamond Lady

18 Small change

19 Small Boys'
20 A Cat
21 Elephant
22 A Ship
23 A House
24 Mouth
25 Big House
26 Bees
27 A Dog
28 Herring
29 Small Water
30 M'fondesi, a chicken, a fowl
31 A Fire
32 Gold Money
33 Little Boy
34 Pudding
35 A Big Hole
36 A Stick

"Haai, I have to play twenty-nine today," Lilian might have said to Shaye, the youngest son, as he unlocked the back door after she rapped on his bedroom window to wake him and let her into the house.

"I had a dream of Small Water, I have to play it, tickey, perhaps sixpence."

There was no formalized publication of the results of the lottery, and even the method for picking the winning numbers was a product of mythology and rumor. No one knew the process, yet, bets were placed, the winning number passed by word of mouth from one backyard to the next, the winning prize money always paid out, and all the servants knew it as 'Farfi', and that 'The Chinaman' was in charge.

...~...

Chapter 10

Thursday?

FRIDAY? Thursday? Was it Thursday? On Thursdays, the second maid would take on Lilian's duties because Lilian was 'Off'.

Thus, the second maid would answer the single ring of the bell and the double ring of the bell that was her usual call.

If the Madam knew it was the head maids' day off, then she knew it was either the second or fourth Thursday of the month. She could have just rung the bell twice and the second maid would have responded.

But she wasn't aware if it was the second or the fourth Thursday of the month or if it was Thursday at all. Her only sign that it was any particular day was when the second maid responded to the single bell instead of Lilian. That meant it was Thursday, either the second Thursday or the fourth Thursday of the month, but a Thursday.

Any day Lilian responded to the single bell, it wasn't either the second Thursday or the fourth Thursday of the month, it was some other day.

The Madam didn't have to instruct the servants on adhering to this exchange procedure. She wasn't aware of how they communicated this procedure to each other. Or how they arranged whose turn it was to be 'off', who knocked on the outside window of the children's bedroom to be let in through the back door of the house in the early morning, and many other details that went into the running of the household.

Sometime during the week, the Madam rang the bell next to the bed three times to call the garden boy.

As she waited for the servant to respond, she reached for the novel and glasses that lay next to her bed and read. Her eyes had weakened over the years, both from poor nutrition and overexertion in dim lighting. A Doctor might have ventured an analysis that all the pills and her diabetes contributed something to the condition and her mother might have contributed, "Finish your carrots, it's good for the eyes."

When the garden boy responded with a gentle knock at the bedroom, she would drew the silken ribbons of her sheer pink bed jacket tightly around her throat and conveyed her instructions to him while holding the ribbons, her heavy hand falling and rising on her ample breasts hidden beneath her nightgown.

…❧…

THE Madam never attempted to conceal her intimate femininity in front of the children. Occasionally, she would stand naked in front of the full-length mirrors of her wardrobe, and dress, unembarrassed by her son's embarrassment at the bedroom door.

She started, or continued a conversation while pouring her body into the large pink corset, or 'two-way', as she referred to it.

She pulled the corset easily to the level of her knees, but from that point, it turned into an intricate and occasionally desperate struggle.

…❧…

SHE had gone to the hospital for the birth of her first child, totally unaware of the process of childbirth. She endured the pain of natural childbirth with such ample degrees of terror and wonder that it made one ponder whether her first sexual experience as a virgin with her husband had perhaps approached the same intensity, and had perhaps evoked the same feelings.

Her stomach, that pink ribbed fold of skin with luminescent lines reached to her knees.

Her stomach,

… distended by three pregnancies, lay over her thighs, concealing that dark triangle of desire that drew her husband to her so many years before.

… that unfilled pit, that drew her inexorably to the refrigerator, once, twice, four, ten, fifteen times a day, was the center of her motivation, her foil against realization, her pet poodle, her stamp collection, her night on the town, her celebration of dedication.

… that eventually wore her teeth down to small yellow stubs, that turned her tongue white and cracked, that turned a willowy young girl into an inflated caricature of the same, that would never ignore her, that would never give her rest.

… that her child blamed himself for creating despite her reassurances to him years later that it was not his fault.

… that floated before her, shiny and transparent in the cold water of the bathtub as she screamed silently and sobbed, trapped, all those years later after her surgery for colon cancer.

… that prevented her reaching the stopper of the bathtub that would drain the water she had been lying in for two hours while her anger swelled, her fear and frustration rose and fell, her thoughts raced and collided as she determined to leave her husband after 40 years, for leaving her this way, abandoned to her stomach in the cold bath water.

… that resisted enclosure like ever expanding foam as she stuffed it inch by inch into the corset while her young son watched the multiple images of her in the wardrobe mirrors as the nausea crept from his stomach, up his windpipe and into his mouth filling it with bitterness, until eventually all the flesh captured, enveloped in elastic and spines and she was ready to present herself to the world with her concealed sheath of shiny armor, impervious to protrusions that surrounded her, cocooned in a web of tension ready to explode, yet safe within the knowledge of her perceived perfect invincibility.

. . . ☙ . . .

THE Madam read almost constantly in-between waking in the morning and going to sleep at night, moving occasionally from one room to another. She started in the bedroom, then to the study, then to the breakfast room for lunch, to the study again, to the breakfast room again for supper, and finally to the bedroom again and sleep.

She passed through the bedroom several times during the day on her way to her bathroom. At those times, the bedroom wasn't recognizable to her in its usual dark emptiness.

In some miraculous manner, as if by a button push from some remote location, the curtains were drawn aside allowing the bright light to enter the room. Stark light only slightly filtered by gossamer sheers detailed the large rolled quilt cushion with a tassel on each end that now lay at the head of the bed.

The plates, cups and glasses, the residues of her late-night visits to the refrigerator, were removed from beside her bed, as perhaps had one more strip of chocolate from the drawer of the bedside table on her husband's side of the bed.

The wardrobe doors were all closed now, multiplying the dimensions of the room and revealing a strangely darkened and segmented but otherwise perfect replica of the bed in its multiple mirror surfaces.

Each time she passed on her way to the bathroom she glimpsed herself as she appeared and disappeared, appeared and disappeared, appeared and disappeared, appeared and disappeared and then with a slight shock, would find herself about to enter the dressing room with its Vibromatic from America and the Beretta pistol on the top shelf of her husband's built-in cupboard.

. . . ☙ . . .

"I need you to go to the library."

"Yes, Madam", the garden boy replied as he moved in the dim light towards the side of the bed only to be halted mid-stride.

"But tell the Madam not the same as last time, different, OK?"

"Yes Madam", he replied as he bent to retrieve the novels stacked under the night table next to the Madams bed, and then exited the room.

. . . ~ . . .

THE night table on her husband's side of the bed matched the Madam's just as it matched the deep cream wardrobe with the full-length mirrors that lined one wall of the room. At the corners of its doors gold scrolls stood in relief, together with similarly accented outer edges and drawers.

The quilted bedcover matched the quilted headboard covered in transparent but yellowing and brittle plastic with a brutal gash just above the stain of Vitalis on her husband's side of the bed, the product of the oils and various medications for psoriasis the Master used.

Instead of washing his hair more often or getting a prescribed medication, he had taken to mixing a concoction suggested by the pharmacist who delivered the medications on Fridays. This involved a mixture of liquid Vaseline or glycerin, Detol, an antiseptic, and witch-hazel. He sprayed the mixture onto his hair each morning before the usual application of either a gel, cream or lotion, invariably, Vitalis or Brylcream.

Neither he nor the Madam bathed very often. Eventually the medication, together with the various hairdressings, formed a layer of its own on the scalp. This dry and cracked layer, floated down to their shoulders where it formed a wide collar of white haze that both wore each day.

Neither of them thought to have the plastic fitted to the headboard. Most of the décor in the house was the doing of the previous owners. The concealed fluorescent lighting, the velvet wallpaper, the ship's prow, the bidet, the bell under the carpet, these were all design touches by the previous owners who had moved 'up' to another neighborhood.

The Madam and her husband had purchased the house with most of the furniture, and curtains included. So it remained for the entire period of their residence besides for a few pieces of furniture and the large head painted on the wall by her son's artist friend that revealed itself after the fire that the garden boy, drunk as he was, had supposedly started and that burned the entire house down.

The house had burned only eight weeks after the Madam and her husband sold the house and returned to the country where she was born, the country that she ignored, that he pined for, driven to find a sense of place and commitment, a place of appreciation and involvement, home, but unknown to him just another stop on that miserable journey to 'France'.

For her husband, the move to the new house had been a symbol of his success. They had moved from one suburb to another, less than half a mile from the first, but separated by thousands of miles in social stature, in that all-important view that was defined by how others viewed you and your family, how the actions of one member of the family reflected on either or both the Madam or her husband.

...❧...

REBECCA'S Secret: She took a chocolate from the drawer in the night table next to the Masters' bed.

Nathan's Secret: He took a chocolate from the drawer in the night table next to the Masters' bed.

Shaye's Secret: He also took a chocolate from the drawer in the night table next to the Masters' bed.

Another Master's Secret: He knew the children were taking his chocolate from the drawer in the night table next to his bed.

...❧...

Chapter 11

The Other (I)

HOW you are perceived by others was the most important factor that influenced their lives.

For the Madam, this perception was a unique melange of multi-layered concepts, premonitions, deceptions and rumors, topped by a certain anxiety and sadness that wholly obliterated, or rather, to a large degree, obscured her own sense of Self.

The only Self she came to know was the Other. That Other person, that constructed Other, that Other she thought others viewed as her Self. That Other that she could never confront. That Other that she could never confirm nor refute. That Other that she had no desire to confirm or refute, so tenacious was its hold on her. That Other, that in fact didn't even remotely align with the view that her neighbors, her friends, her sister, her husband, her maids, and most importantly, her Mother, held of her.

For her husband, the Master, purchasing the house with all the furniture included meant he was not merely buying the space, the structure, the bricks and mortar. He was absorbing the aesthetic, the symbols of status, making them his own, as if these brocade furniture items were his choices, these velvet wall coverings were his dreams fulfilled, his desires met, his vision of delicate design and the accompanying accoutrements. This place supposedly was the castle on the hill overlooking the shtetl, resplendent in its concrete ship's brow with fake portholes, his symbols of success to others.

The husband replaced the whiskey in the Glenlivet bottle with cheap whisky.

They were fooled, and he had fooled them.

Success on all fronts.

...~...

Chapter 12

The Other (II)

THE Other sees Itself.
The Other sees Itself, in Itself.
The Other sees Itself, in Itself, in the Mirror.
The Mirror is Itself.
The Mirror is always not itself.
The Mirror is always itself.
The Mirror never shows itself to itself.
The mirror cannot touch itself either.
Neither does it hear or smell itself.
Then, how does it know it is there?
Is there a clue it can give itself?
Is it itself?
Is it the Other?
Is itself itself?
Perhaps it is.
There is no knowing the Other.
The Other is not sensed.
The Other implies Itself.
The Other is inferred.
The Other is Itself.

...~...

Chapter 13

The Library

THE Librarian at the local sub-branch had a standing request from the Madam.

Some time during the week she rang the bell next to her bed three times to call the garden boy. She then instructed him to return the pile of books that had accumulated beside her bed, and the chair in the study, and exchange them for new ones.

The garden boy could not choose the books, as he barely read English. On entering the library, he would simply place the pile of books on the librarian's desk and stand and wait.

The librarian, without acknowledging the garden boy verbally and with a brief glance at him from above her half glasses, sorted through the books, retrieving the Madam's cards one at a time, piling up the cards on the desk until they tottered over in a multi-colored fan. Red cards for non-fiction, yellow for fiction, the occasional blue for reference books and green for children's books.

The Madam had planned a strategy to satisfy her literary hunger and circumvent the limit of two non-fiction and two fiction books per person imposed by the library. Other than this singular subterfuge, she was, practically, a wholly honest person.

The Madam achieved her literary goal by maintaining the validity of all the family's library cards even though no one besides the Master, the maids, the garden boy, and Shaye lived at the address any longer.

The Master only read the newspaper at the dinner table.

The maids read only the occasional passage from the Bible.

The garden boy struggled to read his 'Passbook'.

In this manner, by these defaults, as she wasn't interested in non-fiction, she had ten cards available, and she used all of them at every request.

She never requested any specific book titles. At the beginning, when she moved into the neighborhood, she had done so, but that quickly faded. She soon found that being a public library, they almost never had that recently published book that was recommended by that friend on the phone just the other day.

She had never purchased a book even though she spent every day reading at least some part of some book. The recommended book was an elusive quest which she eventually triumphed over as a trophy of sorts, when, at some point, one of her friends actually lent her the book, or perhaps when, months, or sometimes years later, by pure chance or coincidence, the librarian included that title in the weekly selection, whereupon the Madam, in her usual subdued manner, reveled in private joy and satisfaction.

The librarian's standing instructions, written in that brief note some years previously, were to fulfill quantity, not quality or specificity. The Madam had worded the note politely yet in sufficiently vague terms as to allow multiple interpretations of her intent. She hid often in this way.

Sometimes the Madam would provide the librarian with some clues by subdividing returned books into two categories, the 'liked' and the 'didn't like' categories. She did this in the vain hope that the librarian would glean some idea of her preferences over the weeks, months, and years of these weekly returns.

Most times, the librarian had the right to choose which fantasies she would absorb for the following week.

The garden boy, a man around thirty years old, had little idea of what this weekly ritual was all about. Most often, the 'liked' and the 'didn't like' piles merged in the basket he hung from the handlebars of the bicycle. To him, this was a good excuse to take one child's bicycle and meet some of his friends or, with some luck, some single girl along the way.

It also served as a reason to get away from the house and stop at the liquor store to buy a short bottle of brandy from the back door of the liquor store, which he would consume out of a brown paper bag behind a tree or fence.

The brandy, not the books, became a daily ritual for him and what eventually led to the rumor that it was he, in an alcoholic daze, had caused the house to burn to the ground just one month after the Madam sold it.

It was a common practice for the servants to 'go with the house' when a property was sold. In the Madam's case, the garden boy 'went with the house', while Lilian 'went with her sister' and the second maid just 'went', 'somewhere'.

When the garden boy returned from his various alternative routes to the library, the maids warned him of the various numbers of times that the bell had rung, inquiring after his absence.

The Madam suspected the garden boy had deviated from her explicit instructions, but her desperation at his lengthy absence served only to increase the expectation of the fulfillment the books would bring. That expectation brought her a kind of satisfaction that was often greater than the satisfaction the books brought to her. She hid often in this way.

Inwardly she was well aware of this need, so when the garden boys' mumbled excuse, was given with downcast eyes and hat in hand, she readily accepted it with no sign of anger or resentment towards him, even though she had endured torturous moments waiting for his return, just as she would continue to juggle desire and need in this fulcrum of injurious satisfaction, until spent and slightly trembling, the Valium would take hold and sleep would obliterate the memory of that conflict.

…❧…

SHE avoided anger as best she could, taking on resentment bitterness and frustration. This was evident ever since she had actually given vent to her full emotion, for the first time, after fifteen years of marriage.

The event that precipitated this outburst was an argument with Nathan. On this occasion, much to her surprise, her normally submissive demeanor erupted in a display of physical and emotional hysteria that ended with two very particular consequences.

The first and most immediate of the consequences was a large bump on Nathan's head, the result of her repeatedly banging his head against the passage wall.

This bump was a peculiar twist of fate, a premonition, a predetermined series of actions, for, over the years, whenever the children complained of boredom or the lack of activities, her reply inevitably would be, "Go and bang your head against the wall!"

These seemingly a-causal events, these points of synchronicity, occurred often and in variety.

The Madam banged Nathan's head against the passage wall.

Shaye banged his head against the wall often and hard, hoping his inner ear pain would disappear.

Lilian, standing behind the Madam at the dinner table drew her finger across her throat.

The farmer standing next to the railway tracks looked at the cattle cars and drew his finger across his throat as the Madam's family peered from between the slats on their way to the concentration camp.

The children stole the chocolate from the Master's drawer.

Lilian replaced the whiskey with tea.

THE second consequence of banging Nathan's head against the passage wall was more enduring than the first, and unlike the electric bell under the dining room carpet, became an integral and often pivotal part of the household's communications with each other.

After banging his head against the passage wall, the Madam ran down the passage, into and across the kitchen, reached into the cutlery drawer in the scullery, and attempted to commit suicide by drawing a large bread knife across her throat in one large and sweeping gesture, followed by several sharp sawing strokes.

Her intrusion totally surprised the servants at various tasks in the kitchen, normally their own domain.

…❧…

LILIAN, leaning over the kitchen sink, a glove and a bracelet of foam at her wrist, her other hand immersed in the lukewarm greasy grey water in the sink, the white plate she held barely touching the bottom.

The second maid with the silverware neatly laid out in rows before her on the yellow Formica countertop, polishing rag in one hand, inverted can in the other, polish dripping slightly from the saturated rag onto the shiny black-and-white checkered floor.

The garden boy sitting on the top stair outside the kitchen door, four and a half pairs of shoes, evenly placed on sheets of newspaper before him, one shoe enclosing his hand like a glove while the other, mid-stroke, holds the worn square polishing brush.

The Madam running screaming "I can't take it anymore! I can't take it anymore!" through the kitchen.

…❧…

Lilian

THE servants were quite used to the various quarrels and arguments in the household. These were completely unlike the family interactions ingrained in their culture before they came to the city to find work.

In this house, usually the disturbances ended in a heavy silence. On those occasions, the servants could go about their daily tasks undisturbed except for taking the occasional surreptitious glance at the sullen silent faces seated at the dinner table.

This time however, the territory around the kitchen sink was intruded upon in a manner unlike any they had witnessed before, even in this strange world they had willingly allowed themselves to take part in. For the first time, the servants enacted and contributed critical parts to the forming of the family's anecdotal history, the mythologies of these lost persons.

Lilian, on seeing the Madam draw the knife across her throat, had wrestled her to the ground, had bowled the Madam over in a tackle at the shoulders.

No, the Madam had collapsed at the weight of Lilian as she grasped her hand at the wrist.

No, the Madam had simply lost her equilibrium in the rush between the imbalance of her thoughts and emotions and limited physical capabilities.

The reality of these moments of the event were a subject of conjecture and a vacillating mythology unresolved.

As Lilian lay on top of the sobbing Madam on the checkered linoleum floor, a peculiar smile grew and then blossomed on Lilian's face until she could barely contain or conceal her mirth and had to roll off the Madam and face the wall, where her laughter became muffled by the bag of potatoes next to the cupboard.

"I just want to die! I just want to die!" the Madam screamed as she entered the kitchen.

Before she reached for the drawer.

Before she reached for the knife in the drawer.

Before she retrieved the knife from the drawer, she had turned the knife to its blunt side before drawing its blunt side across her throat in a sawing motion.

From that moment on, Lilian had a surreptitious means of responding to the many family crises, communicating silently with Shaye seated across the table as she collected the soiled plates.

She stood behind the Madam at the dinner table, pointed at the Madam, drew her finger several times across her throat, and followed the gesture with a silent broad smile directed at Shaye, a smile of understanding, an acknowledgement of the trust and fondness for each other they shared, the seedbed of humor that she revealed to him, his singular joy and alternative from the mire.

This often-repeated scenario was one of the few respites Shaye had from the combination of the tyranny of the Masters pouting or angry silence and the Madam's fog of submission and depression.

The Master ate his dinner behind the evening newspaper. The Madam tracked the path of forks traveling from the children's dinner plates to their mouths. She assessed the quantities of food remaining on plates, while Nathan rubbed his hands raw, ground his teeth and often said, of his younger brother to his mother, "He's disgusting, tell him to wash his hands!" while Rebecca dreamed of her Prince Bennie from that small town far away.

The children learned much and nothing from the wisdom of the servants.

...☙...

Chapter 14

Milked Tea

"COME in!"

It wasn't the second or last Thursday of the month, so two or three minutes after ringing the bell next to her bed, there was a gentle knock at the half-open bedroom door.

"Yes, Madam?"

Lilian entered the semi-darkness of the bedroom to find the Madam as usual, propped up in bed, a small pink lace trimmed pillow inserted behind her neck and an open novel rising and falling on her chest.

In a plaintive, childlike voice, the Madam asked, "What's for breakfast?"

This breakfast ritual was so consistent in all its details that, unknown to the Madam, Lilian had already enacted the complete scenario as she walked down the passageway and at the door before she had entered the room. Lilian was merely performing outwardly what she already knew inwardly.

Redro fish paste on Melba Toast.

Scrambled egg on Melba Toast.

Kippers and egg with a slice of Melba Toast.

Sardines and 2 slices of Melba Toast.

A request for 'A cup of hot, wet tea' always followed the Madam's choice of one of these four options, to which Lilian would always reply with a smile, "Milked or not milked Madam?".

Inevitably, the Madam chose the 'milked' tea, which settled the acid in her early morning sour stomach. Later in the day, when she requested a cup of "hot, wet tea", which she requested a minimum of five or six times a day, she would choose the "not milked" option. The lemon that came with the "not milked" option helped to bite through the layer of chalky residue that had built on her tongue through the day, freeing her taste buds for the onslaught of more taste sensations.

'Milk' or 'No Milk'. What was initially a dilemma had, over time, resolved in the confluence of habit and rationale.

Her body had become a playground of yin and yang. She had to choose between what seemed to be irreconcilable opposites, acid or alkaline, lemon or milk.

The Madam eventually resolved the dilemma by applying the factor of time to the equation. She already knew, if only intuitively, that one plus one equaled three and not two. Process, in her calculation, had become the entire equation, obscuring the individual factors to where they disappeared in the vagaries of the past, where they became confused with fantasies, dreams, and desires.

She needed more than a process to solve the supposed conflict between milk and lemon. She needed time.

Subliminally she was convinced she could always start the day with a cup of 'milked' tea and could follow it up a little later with a cup of 'not milked' tea. This seemed to work well even though the second cup negated the effects of the first, and in fact she was back where she started when she woke up, with a sour stomach.

A surprise benefit of the time that passed between the two cups was, as a result, she could always convince herself that the sour stomach she now experienced resulted from one or more of her physical ailments. With that conclusion in mind, she could now ingest some Eno's Fruit Salts or some Alka Seltzer as the medicinal solution to a medical problem?

...❧...

Chapter 15

The Act of Transference

OVER time, tea was the primary means of initiating various types of interactions with Lilian throughout the day. The Madam used tea to deflect compliments from female guests who would remark on the quality and tastiness of the Maids baking served to them at their intermittent social gatherings or brought along in a biscuit tin to the weekly tennis game. This deflection of a compliment led to the establishment of 'The Act of Transference.'

The Act of Transference begins with the Madam's reply to a guest's compliment, to which the Madam replies, "Well I'll tell you, when she came to us, she couldn't even boil a cup of water, never mind make a cup of tea!" Her friends respond in small titters of understanding.

Her female friends were all affected by the Act of Transference. There was a sense of camaraderie among them, if not a slight tinge of a sense of shared victimization. They communicated this non-verbal understanding to each other aside from the copious verbiage they shared daily on the telephone, about pills, about plastic surgery, about looming menopause.

The Act of Transference meant the Madam could accept the compliments on Lilian's baking by default, implying that by some method she had transferred her abilities to Lilian, a transference that was to be accepted as a matter of cultural normalcy and not really to be examined in conversation.

For males, there was no transference. Food was formal and physical, an unrecognized, central and formative factor in their lives. Many of them bore the imprints of their early childhood experience when some of them almost starved to death or when other family members actually starved to death. When the imprint sometimes bubbled to the surface, that marker of childhood, combined with the nostalgia for innocence or simple pining for the eloquence of history, of times past, it collapsed under the weight of the "Other'.

...❧...

THE men, in a gesture of recognition, perhaps of some kind of prenatal resonance, some distant organic echo of female competence, attempted to compliment their wives or the Madam on the quality of the meal.

Most of the men bore a righteous indignation towards matters in general. With an inflated sense of virulence, they showed a benevolent despotism towards women in general and their wives in particular. That, together with a misguided sense of honesty, practicality and the logical order of events, wouldn't allow them to express themselves adequately. The 'Act of Transference' was one barrier that blocked the way.

The men couldn't direct their compliments correctly to the host without becoming involved in the intricacies of 'The Act of Transference.'

If they attempted to do so, they stood the possibility of making an issue out of what at least initially seemed to be a very simple gesture of politeness. Or, they would have to delve into a mire of details to the point of boring everyone at the table. Or, at worst, they might appear as a Liberal, or a Socialist, or perhaps a Communist!

Cynicism was far more acceptable than liberalism.

Confronted by 'The Act of Transference', the men defaulted on gestures of politeness and deferred to comments of sexual innuendo while continuing their business discussions amongst themselves.

The maids cleared the remnants of the meal they had prepared without so much as a nod of acknowledgement towards their existence from either the Masters or the Madams leaning into the backs of their seats, stuffed and expecting coffee.

…❧…

Chapter 16

Cereal (1)

MEALS, being the central platform for the family's interactions, automatically credited any maid who could cook with the elevated status of head maid.

Any maid who could cook, clean, dust, wash, scrub, baby-sit, iron, understand English, have a legal Pass and not steal the sugar, was at an understandable premium.

This premium never translated into increased wages for the head maid through the dynamism of supply and demand. It simply transformed into the tenacity of each Madams hold on her maid by all means available.

It was only under extraordinary circumstances that a good Head Maid who met all the criteria was available. The word spread throughout the neighborhood rapidly of her availability.

If the Perfect Head Maid was not immediately available through the grapevine, the search found a substitute.

…ঌ…

OVER several weeks, a steady stream of maids knocked on the back gate of the house in response to a grapevine of communication that made the vacancy known amongst the maids of the area. It was a rare occasion that both maids were fired or left simultaneously.

The remaining maid interrupted the family's evening meal to inform the Madam of the prospective applicant's presence at the bottom of the stairs that led from the back door of the kitchen into the backyard.

After dessert, forestalling her usual cup of after-dinner lemon tea, the Madam left the table to question the potential maid at the bottom of the stairs.

…ঌ…

Chapter 17

Cereal (2)

LIGHT spilled from the brightly lit yellow kitchen, silhouetting the bulky frame of the Madam at the top of the stairs. Lilian, sitting on the lopsided stool, merged with the dark background of the yard with its dripping faucet, the mangy mongrel dog Snippy asleep in the corner, and the tin horse lying on its side slightly visible through the door ajar in the crawlspace to the left.

The crawl space under the house remained silent and dank. The tin rocking horse with the broken pedals lay with its nose in the dust, its gilded bridle scratched to bare rusted metal at points, its eyes open in anxious anticipation, or fear, its muzzle frozen in its caricature of joy.

...~...

"YES Nanny?"

"Good evening Madam."

Physical proximity and attitude in this initial encounter were as just as important as any later discussion they might later pursue about 'days off' or 'Christmas pansela'. The height of approximately eight feet from the kitchen door to the concrete of the yard where Lilian stood was a prelude to the emotional distance that was established between them, should the interview conclude successfully. Many times, this distance would collapse and reform, but that initial eight feet would always set the parameters.

Both the Madam and Lilian were familiar with the ritual that was about to take place. Each had already assumed their assigned role and positioned themselves to begin.

The Madam swallowed the encumbrances of the established order and was eager to begin and end Lilian's overture, unlike Lilian, who was nervous at the possibility of unanswerable questions the Madam might have.

It was difficult for the Madam to judge Lilian's responses or if Lilian had any, as the maids always kept their heads lowered and eyes to the ground when they were spoken to.

The maids never looked at her directly for any length of time, but glanced and then looked away in deference. This was disconcerting, but she readily accepted it as this behavior was preferable to any other that might lead to confrontation or argument.

Her presumptions were reinforced when she confronted the illustrations on the back of a box of cereal on the breakfast room table one day. The box of cereal not only opened a new perception of these two traits, but additionally opened a channel to a few other understandings about some previously presumed but now explicit behaviors.

She finally understood the basic tenets of these people who were silent unless addressed and always looked at the ground when addressed.

These behaviors had always seemed peculiar to her, they hadn't intruded on her own behaviors and, in fact, she felt as if they reinforced her status even though she didn't know how, when, or why.

Her status was reinforced whenever she gave the servants some Grandpa Headache powders, or Valium, or when she gave money to Lilian to buy vegetables from the Indian vegetable vendor with the green open-sided truck, or from the Portuguese refugee from Mozambique's store.

Or, when she gave money to the garden boy to buy the plants from the old man with the carrier on the front of the bicycle with the small seedlings individually wrapped in wet newspapers under several layers of burlap.

Or when Lilian asked for money to pay the bread man who had just delivered the hot bread to the back-yard gate, or for the milk-man with the eggs and yogurt.

At any of these moments, Lilian or the garden boy kept their eyes to the ground and put out both hands cupped together, touching at the wrists.

Then they waited, hands outstretched, until they felt the touch of whatever was placed in their hands. At that moment they would reverse the motion of cupping, and without examining what was placed in their hands, saying, as they reversed, "Thank you Madam."

...❧...

Chapter 18

The Back of the Box of Cereal

THE back of the box of cereal illustrated a simple situation dealing with milk, something everyone supposedly understood on some subliminal level and that the junior designer at the advertising agency felt had more than simply a practical relationship with the cereal in the box.

A photograph showed a Madam holding a bottle of milk, with a maid waiting to receive the bottle, hands cupped and eyes to the ground. In an italicized word balloon above the Madam's head, it read, "Here's some milk for you". In another word balloon above the head of the maid read, "Thank you very much".

A bold heading next to the photograph read, 'INTERESTING'.

Underneath the heading, the copy explained;

'It is customary to use both hands when giving or receiving things. Often gratitude is expressed with gestures, a slight curtsey or the clapping of hands.'

The illustration failed to explain why the Madam was giving milk to Lilian but was an acceptable action without query.

Another illustration shows a photograph of a maid on the left and a Master on the right.

In a word bubble above the Masters' head, it read, "Good Morning!"

In a word bubble above the Maid's head, it read, "Good Morning!"

A photograph next to the word bubble showed the Master with a perplexed look, chin resting in his hand, and a word bubble above his head reading, "Why does she look away whenever I greet her?."

The bold title read, 'EXPLANATION'.

Again, under the heading it explained; 'Traditionally, the senior person greets first. It is often a sign of respect to avoid eye contact and not raise one's voice when talking to one's senior.'

To the Madam, the first illustration was very clear and she quickly passed on to the second which perplexed her immediately.

It hadn't been quite clear from the illustration who had addressed whom first. In fact, it appeared as if Lilian addressed the Master first, her being on the left and both word bubbles being of equal size.

She re-examined the illustration once again.

After some moments of contemplation and reconsideration, she concluded the copy had been correct and that the Master had addressed Lilian first.

She drew that conclusion by noting that the designer had crossed the tails of the word balloons so that the balloon of the Master was on the left, even though the Master was positioned on the right.

With a single stroke of inferential logic, she then drew the obvious conclusion that the Master's word balloon being on the left and English being read from the left to right gave priority to the Master.

...❧...

Chapter 19

The Pass is Good

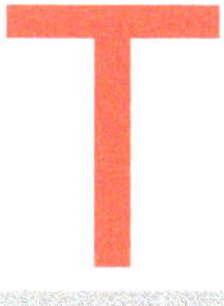

THE point at which this maid looked at her directly wasn't until many years later when Lilian realized the look on the Madams face wasn't one of superiority or reproach, but the countenance of resignation, an attitude that Lilian rarely experienced, if ever, but came to recognize as time passed.

Compassion was a dominant trait of Lilian's culture, and it came easily to her. She could be compassionate without acknowledgement or reward, unlike the Madam who desperately sought acknowledgement as a sign that reinforced her sense of self.

This was a curious reversal of the cultural normalcy imposed on both their roles. By all outward impressions, Lilian should be the one to seek constant reinforcement of herself. Her identity, her culture, her history, every point where her personal life may have touched that of the Madam or her family, was, every day, every hour, completely denied, except by the other servants, who suffered under similar fates.

The Madam, with all the cultural signs of confirmation, affirmation, and validation, was so embroiled in her search for confirmation, affirmation, and validation, and the endless cycle that produced was incapable of the basic rudiments of impulsive compassion.

For the Madam, what often appeared as compassion or understanding to the unobservant was, in fact, her old enemy, and partner, resignation.

...~...

MADAM: "Who sent you?".

Maid: "Madam Hilda, Madam, from Letaba Road Madam."

The Madam and Lilian faced each other to discuss Lilian's potential employment. Or, more accurately, the Madam looked down at Lilian, looking at the ground, to discuss Lilian's potential employment.

Madam: "Can you cook?"

Maid: "No Madam, but I can learn if Madam will teach me Madam."

Madam: "Well, that's not good. Have you got your papers, your pass?"

Maid: "Yes Madam."

Lilian handed over a small brown pass book which she had been holding pressed into the small of her back during the entire conversation. Shiny with perspiration and smelling slightly of soap and camphor, the Madam opened the dog-eared and worn book, checking for the signatures and dates of service of Lilian's previous employers. She paused when she came to the section that stipulated the expiry date of the document.

Madam: "But your pass has expired!"

Maid: "Yes Madam."

Madam: "I can't take you if your pass has expired!"

Maid: "Yes Madam, but Madam can make an application Madam."

Madam: "No, no. If you don't have a pass, they will come and arrest you, you know. And then what will I do? I won't have anyone!"

Maid: "Yes, but Madam, my husband ..."

Madam: "Husband, you have a husband?"

Maid: "Yes Madam, but not married Madam."

Madam: "What do you mean you're not married. He isn't your husband then is he?"

Maid: "Yes, he is Madam, but we can't marry Madam. We are both not allowed in town if we are married, Madam. We can't get pass then Madam. They will arrest us Madam."

Madam: "Yes, but you don't have a pass, anyway. It has expired. Anyway, I can't have two of you living here. That's too many back here. Who's going to pay for his food?."

Maid: "I will Madam. He won't stay here, Madam. He works over there, *lapa* side Madam, Saxonwold, Madam."

Madam: "No, no. I need someone with a pass. This one is no good."

Maid: "Yes, but Madam, I can have a pass, Madam can do the application."

Madam: "But this pass is no good."

Maid: "Pass is good Madam. Madam can apply at De Villiers Street, Madam."

Madam: "No, no, that's too much trouble. You can't cook and I haven't got the time to go to De Villiers Street. I'm sorry, okay? Do you understand then, hey? Okay?"

Maid: "Yes Madam. Can Madam sign for me for this week then Madam?"

Madam: "I can't sign for you for the entire week. I'll sign for you tonight then, okay?"

Maid: "Yes Madam, thank you Madam."

After calling for a pen from the other maid who hovered indistinctly at the periphery, the Madam signed the pass book on the page for permissions to travel and handed back the book. T

Lilian who, after climbing a couple of steps, received the book with both hands cupped together and eyes to the ground.

The Madam turned and left the top of the stairs for the inside of the house, leaving Lilian halfway up the stairs.

No more was said between them. The interview was over.

...❧...

THE interview was over, but their relationship was not. In fact, it was just the beginning of a relationship that would extend over 25 years, where it would intrude and embroil itself in the most intimate details of the Madam's life, where Lilian became her most trusted companion although she was never able to recognize their relationship as such, and which would end on a hill overlooking the city beyond the small lake several decades later.

FOR a week a steady stream of maids came to the bottom of the stairs, but all were unsuitable. Too old, too young, no references, no pass, no English, bad references.

And then the first maid returned to the bottom of the steps.

The Madam was getting more and more desperate, and more and more depressed at not having a head maid.

Her husband had become unusually silent and sullen behind the evening newspaper at the supper table, even refraining from giving his usual intermittent commentary on various current events he was reading while eating.

The remaining maid had been forgetting to bring in the milk and yogurt in the morning from outside the garage side door. In the heat of the oncoming day, it hadn't taken but two hours for it to turn sour.

For three days, the children had gone to school with no cereal and complaints about the butter and jam sandwiches she had hurriedly made for their school lunch.

Her chilblains had been aching, and her varicose veins, her cracked heels and her ingrown toenails, and the large body massager from America was doing nothing to reduce her weight as was promised.

The garden boy brought back an especially slim selection of books from the library, and her memories of the Place de Pigalle and the canals of Venice were fading rapidly.

No consoling from her friends on the telephone could deliver the appropriately qualified maid, despite their own experiences with the same situation. Good maids just weren't to be had, her friends complained in commiseration. The Madam agreed saying, "If they aren't using up all the sugar, they're cooking 'morogo' in the kitchen."

...✑...

Chapter 20

A World of Shadows.

MAROGO was an indigenous and potent smelling vegetable similar to spinach. Normally, the servants would cook 'morogo' in the laundry room, an outhouse separate from the main house. Here they had set up their cooking and eating facilities amongst the sheets, socks, soaps and bleaches, and the large concrete washing tub.

Occasionally a new maid under the stress of having to cook the servant's meal of morogo, mielie meal, and a small amount of 'Boys' meat' on the paraffin fueled 'Primus' brand stove in the laundry room, would use the 6-plate electric stove in the main house to cook a portion of the meal. This inevitably resulted in a word of caution from the other maid, who was reprimanded by the Madam for creating the pungent smell of morogo that permeated the house for hours.

The disappearance of the white sugar was not so easily discernible. The solution to that problem evaded the Madam right up to the point when she left the country and took up Hermesetas, followed by Saccharin, followed by Sweet and Low, followed by NutraSweet, and left her friends to grapple with the disappearance of the white sugar, supposedly to the laundry room for some unknown purpose.

The laundry room was one of several outhouses that were built at the back of and close to the main house and next to the two-car garage where the Master honked for the manservant every night at precisely six-fifteen.

Adjacent was another outhouse divided into 4 sections. In that outhouse were three rooms, approximately eight feet by eight feet, one for each of the servants, each with the optional small window.

The window, set above eye-level, faced away from the house but towards the garbage cans and the high wall dividing the property from the neighbor.

Attached, as the fourth partition, was the combination bathroom and toilet facility comprising a ceramic toilet with no seat and a single cold-water shower head. The water constantly dripped from the shower head onto the concrete floor, leaving a conspicuous broad stain on the otherwise bare and unremarkable concrete floor.

...❧...

EACH day, year in and year out, the Maids could be seen carrying steaming galvanized buckets of hot water through the yard from the laundry room to the bathroom. There they meticulously bathed in the bucket, emerging from the darkness of the bathroom into the dawn of the day, their faces, hair, arms and legs shining from the application of Zambuk or Karoo or Nivea creams, smelling of camphor and mint.

Having dressed, the maids re-emerged resplendent in a pastel dress with white piping along the collar edge, the ends of the short sleeves, the edges of two pockets, and down the front of the front to the waist, alongside four buttons.

A frilly edged apron and headscarves or starched hats matched similarly, the uniform completed by shoes polished to a reflective mirror finish as was the floor of each room, polished to a gleam with either red or green Cobra brand paste wax.

The maids, for reasons unknown to the Family, were never seen bareheaded unless glimpsed through a window or a crack in a door while moving to or from the bathroom in the early morning.

Neither did the family ever see a maid lying in bed, or the bed unmade, or anything but the meticulous order of the room.

They polished the floor of each room to a gleam with either red or green Cobra brand paste wax.

Along the rear wall, under the window, was a single bed. No matter what the time of day, the bed was always impeccably made. Draped over the bed in precise and balanced sequences of shape and design were various starched and hand embroidered white cloths entirely devoid of wrinkles but resplendent in peaks formed by ironing and starching while folding.

Single blankets rolled together with a white embroidered cloth into a bed-width roll were placed at each end of the bed that stood with each hooped metal foot on two empty one-gallon paint containers, such that the top of the bed stood at waist level, far above the concrete floor where the 'tokoloshe' slithered around at night.

In the corner, stretched between two intersecting walls, a piece of wire with yet another embroidered cloth, concealed the small number of articles of clothing that hung from a wooden pole or sometimes another piece of wire stretched across the corner.

Against another wall, between several thin wooden tomato boxes stacked to form shelving, stood a small table with an oilcloth covering, perhaps a candle in a metal holder, and several photographs in stand-up frames. Sometimes one, or perhaps two, small, well-worn metal folding chairs are drawn up to the table at each end.

Lilian lived, entertained, and hosted her own visiting children and those of the Madam. Here she cried, and hoped, but mostly laughed and drank voluminous quantities of 'skokian' with her 'husband' for going on twenty years. Neither the Madam nor the Master ever entered any of the rooms of those outhouses that stood ten feet away from their bedroom door.

In some senses, this was yet another confirmation of the ignorance that prevailed in this society of fleeting ghosts, shadows, and spirits.

Simultaneously the servants rejoiced in the independence of anonymity, where the bosses never knew, nor cared, nor could intrude upon their private lives, their beliefs, or their dreams.

The laundry room, next to a storage room and the filter for the swimming pool, was painted a bright fuchsia, the result of a mistaken paint mixing that couldn't be sold at the family's paint store.

Years of black paraffin soot from the 'Primus' stove that was the servant's only means of cooking had accumulated on the walls, but especially on the ceiling and the undersides of the various cupboards that lined the walls.

Looking into the room from the top of the stairs at the back of the main house, it often appeared to the Madam as if the room, with the blue glow of the hissing 'Primus' stove as its center, was entirely aglow with fire and scurrying demons with fleeting shadows, hiding.

She was unfamiliar with shadows. Her world was filled with the light of concealed fluorescents and multiple incandescent lamps. She was familiar with reflections and refractions. She was familiar with the endless loop created by the multiple mirrors of her wardrobe as she pulled up her corset or as she lay in the large bed, waiting. Not shadows.

...❧...

... the hissing primus stove ...

THE servants were quite familiar, unafraid, yet respectful of shadows.

They knew the moving flickering shadows of a candle as they entered their immaculate rooms or walked to the bathroom to urinate in the middle of the night, across the open courtyard where the dog scratched at fleas at the bottom of the concrete stairs.

They knew the shadow of a single light bulb as the center of a singular universe whose details faded to nothing at the outer reaches.

They knew the shadow of a torch shone into a window in the middle of the night with shouting voices, "Wakker kaffir, wakker!".

They knew the shadow of the bushes where the 'skelems' and 'tsotsi's' waited to steal your pass book and rip open your stomach with the slash of a knife or crack your skull with the stroke of a knobkerrie.

They knew the shadow of the sunset as they walked from suburb to suburb, knowing that the light would soon be gone, that soon the police trucks would be out patrolling, that they had to reach their destination quickly or else endure another beating, another week without pay, another entry on the record.

They knew the shadow of the rising sun and its soft and gentle edges as they carried the buckets of hot water to the bathroom as the new day formed in pink and orange, just as well as they knew the harshness of the midday as the cry went up, "Shaya!", and the light at the edge of the storm feathered the curtain of the oncoming rain.

They knew the shadow of the hissing Primus stove as well as the smell of sour mieliepap mingled with the odor of paraffin, morogo and bleach, and they longed for the glow of warmth from the fire under the pot inside their one-roomed home, out there, many miles away, by the farms.

Their rooms, their histories, were always full of fleeting shadows, either their own or of others. They knew the shadow of the rising sun and its soft and gentle edges as they carried the buckets of hot water to the bathroom as the new day formed in pink and orange, just as well as they knew the harshness of the midday as the cry went up, "Shaya!", and the light at the edge of the storm feathered the curtain of the oncoming rain.

They lived in a world full of shadows.

In winter, the Primus stove added heat to the otherwise unheated laundry room. The heat combined with the left-over heat from the hot water used during the day for laundry, formed a dank atmosphere where the servants ate at the table the manservant had nailed together from the leftovers of the box cart the youngest son had built but had given up on for the lack of wheels.

For the major part of each day the table served as an ironing board, covered with an old green blanket with two white stripes at either end and a large hole edged in brown in the shape of an iron, the result of the Madam ringing the bell insistently and repeatedly one second Thursday of the month.

It wasn't for many years that the Master installed a washing machine in the laundry room where it shared the space with the three chairs, the table the manservant had nailed together and the twin concrete washing tubs. Before that, all the washing was done by hand, leaning over the tubs filled with scalding hot water and scrubbing the fabric against the washboard like ridges molded into the concrete of the tub.

Each day, the children returned from school to find their beds made, the parquet floors newly polished, and their pajamas that had lain on the bedroom floor, neatly folded under their pillows.

Unlike the rest of the family, Nathan changed clothes, sometimes two or three times a day, just as he sometimes bathed 2 or 3 times a day, and washed his hands constantly, particularly on Saturdays.

The other family members bathed irregularly, never wore cologne or aftershave, wore the same clothes for 3 or 4 days at a stretch and simply left their clothes on the floor, or on a chair, or in the bathroom when they were done, only to find them back in the drawer, washed and ironed, the next day.

The servant's own washing was done on another day. The Madam didn't know which day or when during that day, but the washing occurred, evidenced because each day the maids appeared in one of the three pastel outfits the Madam had purchased for them, freshly washed and perfectly starched and ironed.

The servants' own cleaning was done on another day. The Madam didn't know which day, or when during that day, nor did she enquire nor set any rules. Each day their rooms were meticulously presentable with starched sheets, made-up beds and shiny polished floors.

How or when all these personal activities of the servants occurred always remained a mystery to the Madam, as did the mechanizations of Farfi.

The servants worked all day, from the morning six o'clock wake up task when they rapped on the children's window to have them open the back door, to the seven o'clock quitting time when they entered to request someone lock up after them as they closed the back door for the night. A regular thirteen-hour workday determined not by negotiation or discussion, tradition or common cause, but by the completion of tasks.

Sunday was a half day, while every second Sunday was a day off, to go to church or visit friends, and every second Thursday was a day off.

For those days off, aside from the regular thirteen-hour day, the servants often worked 18-hour days or 80-hour weeks when they were told to 'stay in', sometimes twice or three times a week.

'Staying in' meant babysitting so the parents could go out to 'dinner and a show', leaving their children 'safe' with the head maid. That is until 'The Maids Plot' became more than just unfounded speculation and casual rumor.

Once or sometimes twice a week, the head maid babysat for the Madams children until 10 or 11pm. She sat on a blanket placed on the kitchen floor, her own infant child curled up silently asleep beside her, while the Madam's children lay asleep in their bedrooms, down the long passage, past the locked iron gate and the locked glass door, until the Master and Madam returned and they would be 'let out'.

Madam: "Is everything okay?."

Maid: "Yes Madam."

Master: "Okay, goodnight."

Maid: "Goodnight Master, goodnight Madam."

Madam: "Goodnight. Don't forget the milk in the morning!."

Maid: "Yes, Madam."

Madam: "And the Sammy comes tomorrow. You know that, hey? We need it for the weekend."

Maid: "Yes Madam, but we need little, just potatoes and some carrots."

Madam: "Okay then, but you still have enough money from last week then, hey?."

Maid: "I think so Madam, four, five rand more."

Madam to the Master: "Have you got five rand?."

Master: "Here, here's ten, I don't have any smaller."

Madam: "Okay then, that'll be good for a while then. If it's not, just tell the Sammy to put it on the account and we will fix up later than, okay?."

Maid: "Yes Madam."

Madam: "Goodnight then."

Maid: "Goodnight Madam."

...❧...

THE Master closed, locked and bolted the kitchen backdoor behind the retreating maid with the blanket bump on her back, and placed the key on the yellow Formica countertop where it was retrieved at six o'clock the next morning by one child who responded to the Maids knock on their bedroom window so they could be let into the kitchen to prepare the breakfast for the family.

Another day is done.

...❧...

THE 'boyfriend', or 'husband' of Lilian, the father of her only child, spent some nights with her in her room in the courtyard and left furtively at dawn to return, walking, to his room at the rear of another Madam's house some miles away in another suburb.

They couldn't get married. If they did so, the law required one of them to return to the farm or the village where their parents or their grandparents now lived after becoming too old to work in the city. Where they too would live when they grew old.

The servants rarely married, at least formally as recognized by the law and despite the reverence with which their culture held the sanctity of marriage, both in their newer beliefs of Christianity and their traditional beliefs of centuries. To their friends and family, they were married but not in the eyes of the pass laws.

Their nights were often nights of extremes. Laughter and tenderness, passions and ecstasies were often interrupted by the brutal invasion of a pass raid, when the husband would be hauled away, shirtless, humiliated and shivering in the cold night and shoved into the police van with several other men similarly shivering, shirtless and often bleeding from a wound on the head from the blow of a sjambok.

Although his pass was valid, he had been found at a place 'not of his employment', without the required signature from his Master, or his Madam, or one of their children.

Usually he would be sentenced to a fine, the equivalent of a week's wages and would Lilian in jail until his family could gather the money either from their meager savings, or by contributions from various friends, or from playing Farfi, or from that extra two or three rand originally assigned for 'the Sammy'.

Lilian would go to the court to pay the fine, for which she was docked the day's pay by the Madam, or otherwise, Lilian waited until the next 'second Thursday', to have him released from jail so she wouldn't be docked the day's pay.

Another day is done.

...~...

Chapter 21

Why the White Sugar Disappeared

MADAM: "Yes."

Maid: "I came to see if Madam found someone, Madam."

Madam: "No, not yet."

Lilian remained silent at the bottom of the stairs, hands behind her back, clasping the small brown book, eyes to the ground.

It took a few moments for the Madam to realize that Lilian wasn't about to say anything in response to her comment.

Madam: "Oh well, what was your problem then, hey?"

The Madam couldn't separate or remember one Maid from the other. What she perceived, what was her priority at that moment, was utility, not personality.

In an extraordinary cultural leap of inference, Lilian, understanding this, responded to the Madam's question by simply climbing the few steps to reach the Madam with an outstretched hand, and handed over her small brown book. She then retreated, regaining her initial pose, eyes to the ground, at the bottom of the steps.

The Madam slightly taken aback paged through the book, pausing momentarily to ask:

"Who was it that sent you again?"

Maid: "Madam Hilda Madam, from Letaba Road, Madam."

Madam: "And why did she let you go?"

Maid: "No Madam, it's my sister Madam, she is working for Madam Hilda, Madam."

Madam: "Oh."

Seeing that everything in the book was in order up to that point, the Madam's hopes were rising. "A bit young, only eighteen. I hope she can handle the kids", she thought to herself as she squinted at the details of the book.

Madam: "And you're not pregnant, are you?"

…~…

AN image had suddenly arisen in the Madam's fertile imagination. She had employed several Maids over the years who had gone about their daily work, scrubbing floors, carrying loads of laundry with their newly born child strapped to their backs enveloped in a blanket.

Or at least she presumed it was a child, she never asked and the Maids never offered any explanation for the bump under the blanket. The Madam never heard the baby cry nor saw the baby's face.

It was a curious phenomenon how the children of the maids were born. At some point, Lilian's pregnancy would become just too obvious as she was about to reach the term.

Having delayed as much as possible, Lilian approached her Madam to ask for leave to have the baby. The Madams often reacted with shock, and often with irritation, and often with anger. Paying Lilian during her absence was a prerogative of the Madams and depended on many factors, none based on regulation or custom.

Their responses weren't necessarily guided by any of the moral implications they might have applied to similar news from their own daughter, or about their neighbor's or a cousin's daughter, or a niece.

They knew the maids were not married, and they tolerated the glimpses they caught of the various males as they entered or exited the Maids' rooms. They were mainly concerned about the disruption of the regularity of the household for the month-long absence of Lilian.

After meeting the Madam's requirement for her to find a replacement for the period of her absence, Lilian returned to the village, usually where her mother lived, to have the baby.

On the assigned day of her return, the family in the house was greeted at the breakfast table by Lilian as if nothing had happened besides the disappearance of her large stomach and the appearance of a large bump on her back covered with a blanket as the family went about their breakfast as usual.

No-one asked to see the child, there were no congratulations, or if there had been a miscarriage, no words of consolation or concern for the maids health.

...❧...

THE maids ate their meals in the fuchsia laundry and worked from six am to seven pm, seven days a week, except for every second Thursday and every alternate Sunday to go to church.

The maids carried the steaming hot water from the laundry room to the bathroom in the galvanized bucket.

The maids room contained the single bed set on the upturned paint cans, and the small table with two chairs.

The Primus stove hissed and blackened the walls of the laundry room.

The child remained on Lilian's back in the blanket.

The garden boy exchanged the books at the library.

The bell under the carpet in the dining room remained unused.

Until, one day, the bump on Lilian's back disappeared.

Which day exactly, or which week was a mystery unknown to the Madam and her family, as was the bump's name, gender and to where it had disappeared.

The only clue to any of this the Madam might have noticed, was the increase or decrease in the disappearance of the white sugar.

Other than the sugar, there remained no indicator nor evidence of the child's presence, past or future.

...~...

Chapter 22

Cholent and Gribbenes

MADAM: "But your pass has expired!"

The Madam had come upon the page she had seen several days ago.

Maid: "Yes Madam."

Madam: "I can't take you if your pass has expired!"

Maid: "Yes Madam, but Madam can make an application Madam."

Madam: "No, no, I need someone with a pass. This is no good."

Maid: "Pass is good Madam. Madam can make an application at De Villiers Street Madam."

Madam: "No, that's too much trouble. Can you cook?"

Maid: "No Madam ... but ..."

Madam: “You can’t cook either? And I don’t have the time to go to De Villiers Street.”

Maid: “But I can learn to cook Madam. I can read English Madam. I passed standard five Madam.”

Madam: “I don’t need reading, I need cooking.”

Maid: “Yes Madam.”

The Madam stood at the top of the stairs anticipating the retreat of Lilian. Lilian remained standing at the bottom of the stairs, silent, eyes to the ground, her hands clasped behind her back.

Lilian’s repeated agreement with almost every expressed conclusion of the Madams had the effect of simply reflecting the Madam's opinions of herself, at herself. Each ‘Yes, Madam’ reflected her frustration and her constant effort to make practical conclusions in the face of her husband’s constant criticism.

Her head hurt and she wondered if this was the onset of another of her blinding migraine headaches, the same pain she felt when she couldn’t find her glasses as she strained to read her current novel in the darkness of the bedroom.

Madam: “Okay then, come on Thursday ..., no, come on Friday, yes, Friday, that will be better. We will see if we can fix your pass then. Okay, Nanny?”

She referred to Lilian as ‘Nanny’ because she couldn’t remember Lilian's name.

She did remember that it was Thursday, and this was the day the other Maid was ‘off’. She couldn’t have gone to DeVilliers Street even if she had the will or energy. Without having one of the maids available to “look after the house while I’m gone, okay?”, she didn’t feel secure enough to leave the house to fend for itself.

She had to think of what or where the family would eat out that night. She certainly wasn’t going to cook. She demanded the servant’s cooking skills because she herself possessed no such skills.

Not that she didn’t have the skills or the intelligence or the patience. She had just given up, resigned, reconciled to living with potential's undirected, latent abilities like many of her desires and needs, left at the countertop of unattended service, but for the maids..., and her mother.

Occasionally on a Friday evening, and always at the high holy days, the Madam's mother would come over and supervise the cooking of the meal. Lilian and the Bobba would stand at the stove, pots boiling and steaming, roasts in the oven, desserts and fish dishes congealing in the refrigerator, cookies and cakes cooling on the countertops.

…☙…

THE menus varied very little, confined to a melange of traditional and pseudo traditional items.

Pickled herring: Herring pickled with onions and sugar, served segmented in finger size bits and eaten on matzo crackers.

Chopped Herring:

Pickled herring ground finely and mixed with sugar, tart apple, eggs, white bread, cider vinegar and oil.

'Danish' Herring:

Chopped herring with the addition of Tomato sauce.

Pizah:

A concoction of fish brawn mixed with gelatin and garlic topped with sliced boiled eggs.

Gefilte Fish:

A cake of chopped white-fleshed freshwater fish, carp or pike. mixed with onions and carrots, celery, parsley, eggs and matzo meal. Boiled in broth for a while and served cold with red horseradish and garnished with a slice of boiled carrot balanced on top.

Chopped liver:

Pate of chicken liver served on a platter topped with boiled eggs crumbled into separate white and yellow segments. Presented on a platter in a pattern, usually the Star of David or several segments like a dartboard, or else simply four quadrants, all depending on the mood of Lilian that day.

Kneidlach:

Dumplings, soft and large, filling the soup bowl almost side to side, floating in a transparent chicken soup distilled from hours of boiling a whole chicken together with the bones and necks and feet of at least another chicken until the flesh falls off the bones and disintegrates into the mix of whole onions, sticks of celery and cloves of garlic.

Latkes:

Potatoes shredded and expunged of all moisture and deep fried until crispy brown. Served with a topping of sour cream sprinkled with white sugar.

Lokshen:

Flat Noodles added to chicken soup and kneadlach.

Perogen:

Triangles of soft dough with a beef filling added to chicken soup, kneidlach and lokshen. Also, baked in a pastry dough with a brushing of egg and served with the main dish.

Tzimmes:

A brisket stewed with prunes, carrots and potatoes.

Cholent:

Any mixture of meats and vegetables cooked at the lowest possible heat for extraordinarily long periods resulting in taste-infused blobs of dark brown artifacts and weighing twice as much as their initial or presumed weight, defying their complete consumption at any one sitting.

'Chinese' chicken:

Simply a whole chicken baked in the oven with chunks of pineapple and served over a bed of white rice.

Beef tongue:

Doused in a sweet clear sauce of yellow sultana raisins and served whole on a platter so everyone could fight over who would get the tip.

Leg of lamb:

Roasted at first in a very hot oven and then very slowly at medium heat so that the thin fatty skin of the leg is crispy to the bite and the flesh remains soft and dripping juices from fork to mouth.

Gribenes:

The left-over chicken skin after being fried with chopped onions to liquefy the fat into 'schmaltz', drained of the emulsified 'schmaltz' and served mixed in mashed potatoes or chopped liver.

Yellow squash or pumpkin:

Grilled with sugar and cinnamon.

Roasted potatoes:

Boiled, sometimes twice, and then baked in the oven until crispy golden brown on the outside and fluffy white on the inside.

Carrot salad:

Grated carrots with a fresh orange juice and sugar dressing.

Kugel:

A side dish of flat egg noodles baked within a mix of sweet and sour creams and cheeses with raisins.

Blintzes:

Squares of sweet dough filled with several sweet and sour cheeses and fried or baked.

Hamantaschen:

The 'Ears of Hammen', pastries filled with honey infused poppy seeds.

...❧...

THE occasion of the high holy days drew the entire family together, or, at least it drew the Madam's family together to the same place for that one day a year when the formal dining room was used, as was the bell under the burgundy carpet.

The Master hadn't spoken to his brother, Issac, for over twenty years over a supposed cheating at a card game and both his parents had passed on, so no one in his family was present at the table.

The Madam's brother, Lennie, and her sister, Betty, their wives and husbands and young children, lived close by, as did her mother. They made the trip once a year to Betty's or Lennie's house just as she, the Madam, made the trip to their house for the second night, or the breaking of the fast.

Every year there were several calls between the siblings coordinating the various suppers required of the high holy days, each call confirming the memory of the last miserable occasion and deferring to the priority of the next of kin to host that years first night, or second night, or last night, depending on the order that was established in prior years.

The Madam's children were much older than those of Lennie and Betty. Much of her children's teenage ventures into sex, the admissions of homosexuality, drugs and independence, were translated by her yet inexperienced brother and sister, as being the failing of the Madam both as a parent and mother, further confirming their negative opinion of the Master as parent, father and husband.

Some years later, Lennie and Betty had their challenges with their children, but they never acknowledged this to the Madam who would have been uplifted by the most minimal gesture of understanding and kindness.

Penniless and almost immobile with depression, her courage at finally leaving her husband, never pricked the consciousness of her mother, of Lennie, or of the other ladies, except for her last childhood friend, Hilda, the proud wife of her Communist husband with the Volvo and the sole friend to attend the unveiling of her tombstone.

…❧…

Chapter 23

Show and a Dinner

DINNER and a show. La Fontainebleau. The Station. Prawns. Kosher. Taiglach. Pitzah. It was 1958. It was Thursday. Her mind raced with various options. She had to think about where the family would eat out that night. Perhaps she could call some friends for a recommendation.

Eating out was rare because Lilian always made sure there was a prepared dinner in the refrigerator for Thursday's, her day off.

This search for a maid was proving to be an unending and frustrating quest.

The family hadn't eaten out in years. The few times the family had gone out to eat together was usually on the occasion of a birthday. On those rare occasions, they had gone to the main railway station to dine on a standard prix fixe menu. That way they could order repeated servings of any one item and often several orders of the custard and peach dessert, or vanilla ice-cream and pears.

…❧…

DINNER and a show.

The family never attended a movie together.

In fact, they had attended no cultural events together besides for the African mine dances they took several visiting dignitaries or distant relatives to view.

It wasn't until many years later that Shaye wheeled his mother into a cinema matinee, where they sat together at the rear of a cinema, she in the wheelchair, looking down the twin tracks of lights embedded in the floor at the foggy screen image of Julia Roberts through her fingerprinted and greasy eyeglasses, and he, unable to focus through the tears, hid in the darkness from his mother and the two other vague figures some rows ahead in the cinema that day.

Actually, the ritual was 'Show and Dinner' although she and her friends always referred to it as 'Dinner and a Show'. Actually, most of her friends never referenced that ritual at all anymore. They had in the past, and when they had, they had done so with positive acknowledgement, if not genuine enthusiasm, at the idea.

'Dinner and a Show' or 'Show and Dinner', was a Saturday night ritual, the one night of the week assigned by all the women to maintain actual physical contact with the friends they spoke to on the phone daily.

The two couples met at the local cinema where their children had left the residues of their urine soaked shorts, their empty bottles of pineapple flavored 'Hubbly Bubbly' and the echoes of E–N-O, a mere 2 or 3 hours earlier.

The women had already decided what movie they would see, and the choice always bore the men. These were women's movies. They were much more taken with Cowboys and Indians, spies, or war. Their lack of exposure to other alternatives did not halt their criticism of the women's choices. Cultural phenomena like literature or films just never entered conversations between them. Their conversations almost always centered on sex or business.

That didn't matter too much because later, after the 'Show', after they had eaten 'Dinner', the two men would excuse themselves from the table and head towards the men's toilet.

…❧…

"THIS one's mine," one man would say to the other as they stood at the porcelain urinals.

"No, no, this one's on me," the other responded.

"No, no really, this one's on me."

"No, shit, what are you a fucking millionaire!"

"No! Are you?"

"If you're a fucking millionaire, it's because you're fucking cheating and you're going to pay all the dinners from now on!" the other replied, chuckling.

"Fuck you! You're cheating, bloody ganef! You're just fucking jealous! You couldn't count to a fucking million, never mind make a fucking million! You're just like a kaffir, heh, heh!," the other countered, laughing.

"That reminds me, hey. Did you hear the one about the kaffir and the genie?," replied the other.

"Shit, man, not another genie. Did you hear about the genie who…?."

"Wait man, listen to this one, you'll piss yourself man."

"I'm already pissing, man!"

"Fuck that man, listen. There's this kaffir you see, and he's going through the rubbish dump, hey. So, he picks up this oil lamp. It looks pretty good, like it's worth something, like a shilling, dumb kaffir you know, it's probably worth like a pound or more, but fuck, he doesn't know. Anyway, so he's standing there, fucking bats all around, shit up to his knees and he's rubbing this fucking thing clean. Suddenly, hey, fuck, there's a big puff of smoke and fuck wouldn't you know it, but a fucking genie!"

"He was rubbing his cock! He wasn't rubbing the lamp, he was rubbing his fucking cock!"

"Your cock maybe! Never mind that man. So, this genie says to the kaffir, 'Master (funny hey!), you can make three wishes. What is your first wish?"

"He wants to fuck your wife!!!!!! Ha Ha Ha!!!!"

"No man, shut up man, listen. So, the kaffir says, 'I want my family to have food for all their lives!' Shit, man. Bam! Fuck! There it is. All the food you could want. Shit, the kaffir is amazed. He didn't believe it before, but now he sees its real. "So now Master, what is your second wish?' the genie asks him."

"He wants to fuck your wife!!!!!! Ha, Ha, Ha!!!!"

"Fuck you! Leave my wife out of this. You only wish!!!!"

"You wish. When was the last time you had some cunt, hey! I'll bet you haven't had any for a long time, except that ghatis secretary of yours. Are you still giving her a tup? I wouldn't mind."

"Listen man! Listen! So, the kaffir got the hang of it now hey, so he says to the genie, 'I want a big house, a big house with a bathroom with gold taps, and a swimming pool with a fountain, and a tennis court, and two Mercedes in the garage!' Boom, there's the explosion, and smoke, hey, and there it is, house, swimming pool, tennis court and shit, two big black Mercedes, 250 model, hey!"

"Shit, it would be a 250 for the kaffir!"

"Okay, so the genie comes now to the kaffir and says, 'Okay, you have one last wish. What is it?' So, the kaffir thinks and thinks, and he thinks and he thinks, until finally, with a big smile, he says to the genie, 'I know what I want for my last wish.' 'What is it?' asks the genie. So, the kaffir says, 'I want to be a white man!'."

"No Shit!"

"No, really, he says he wants to be a white man!"

"Bullshit!"

"Boom! Flash! Man, when the smoke clears, there he is, a white man! 'Fantastic, Gott sei dank', he thinks. But then he looks up, he looks up and sees that everything is gone, the food, the house, the Mercedes, all gone!"

"Dafke!"

Now he has his friend's full attention.

"So, he says to the genie, 'Hey, what happened? You fucked up. I'm a white man now, but what happened to everything else, hey? What happened to the Mercedes and everything?' So, the genie turns to him and says, 'No, no, I didn't fuck up. You're white, you're a white man now! Now you have to work for it!!!!',… Good, hey?"

"Schvantz!"

…❧…

Chapter 24

Precarious Balances

"DID he at least offer to pay?"

They lay in bed now. Lilian had been let out. The polyester clothes hung from the chairs in the bedroom as if dripping wet. They both noticed the shadow of the palm tree in the circular window unbeknown to each other.

"Yes", the Master replied vaguely.

"Well, did you settle?" the Madam countered, pressing her inquiry.

"Yes", the Master replied sleepily, irritated at her insistence.

. . . ❧ . . .

Standing at the urinal, both men stared at the glistening stream that connected them similarly to the chrome and porcelain vessel in front of them. As they both breathed hard through their noses, a spreading splash of dark yellow urine pummeled the white porcelain in front of them in a downward cascade, accompanied by a shower of airborne droplets at the point of impact.

…❧…

"WE need to settle for the last time."

"We haven't settled yet."

"I need to settle with you."

"It's time to settle."

The ritual was a part of the alleviation of obligation just as much as it was a vague gesture towards a by-gone cultural code of honor or honesty.

…❧…

MOST of the friends of the Master saw themselves as self-made men, just as he did. Men who had come from situations of abject poverty and now lorded over independent business enterprises. In that quest, the men had learned never to place themselves under any obligation to any one person at any time or for any lengthy period. It was far more helpful to have a debt in your favor, or, if not in your favor, then at least at even status.

This was the advantage of wealth, power and success, and they worked as much at maintaining this status quo as they did at impressing each other, period.

This approach had several negatives.

Outside of the secrecy of the men's various sexual trysts with each other's wives, or the Syrian hardware dealers' daughters, or their secretaries or cashiers, the men carried this kernel of self-preservation close to the vest. The men remained lonely and secretive to where their wives were unaware of the major portion of their daily lives.

Similarly, the men were unaware of the major portion of their wives' lives, and the wives were equally unaware of the lives of the servants. In this secrecy, all parties were equal.

Unless the Madam was interviewing a maid for a job. Then the veil of secrecy only parted long enough to allow the details of identity passes and cooking to percolate through.

…❧…

Chapter 25

Capri

ON the assigned Friday, as arranged, Lilian arrived early in the morning, waiting in the fuchsia laundry room for the Madam to exit the rear door of the house.

The Madam came down the stairs some two hours later, bag hanging from her wrist and keys dangling from her hand, the sound of her polyester petticoat and dress swishing slightly against each other in the silence of the concrete courtyard.

Lilian, in deference to her assumptions, presumed she was to follow and silently shadowed the Madam through the door and into the garage. The Madam and Lilian both opened the front and rear doors, respectively. They both sat down, facing forward. In a singular motion, with a singular echo of sound, as if in a ballet where they were in a perfectly choreographed synchronization of rehearsed motion, they both closed their doors. This was going to be a good day.

The Madam looked in the rear-view mirror to reverse out of the garage.

The Madam screamed.

…⁂…

Chapter 26

Proportional Combinations

THE Madam's fears had finally reached fruition. Here it was. It was happening, here, in this most unexpected location, in her garage with the black oil stain on the concrete floor, in her yellow Zephyr, on a Friday, without warning.

She had imagined it being announced on the radio.

She had imagined it read by her husband from the evening paper.

She had imagined it happening in her bathroom while brushing her teeth.

She had imagined it happening while in bed.

But not here, not now.

Not now.

Why this, why here, why now?

The answer never came. Alone, in the piercing silence of the faded echo of closing car doors, she faced 'The Maid's Plot'.

All she could do was scream and scream. Scream just like she had at hearing of her father's death, just like she had done that day when she bashed her son's head against the passage wall and then ran into the kitchen, just as she had done that day alone in the bath.

All she could do in response to the 'The Maids Plot' was scream and scream repeatedly.

This form of 'The Maids Plot' was ingenious. It overcame all the security measures that were part of the norm in building codes. It overcame all the idiosyncratic additions that each successive homeowner had added to the security system over the years. It overcame all the paranoid defenses that various personalities had imagined or imagined and implemented, erected in the name of peace of mind.

When the Madam purchased the house, the metal bars on every opening of the house seemed a romantic, decorative addition to the general décor. The curving bars forming scrolls of faux vine tendrils covering the windows impressed as much as the scrolls embossed into the velvet wallpaper, and the tassels hanging from the valences in the living room, where no one sat for any length of time.

When she moved with her husband back to the country where she was born, three weeks after they sold the house, the house mysteriously burned down. Everything burned, including all the furniture and ornamentation that she had included in the sale.

The rarely used furniture in the living room, the bell under the burgundy carpet and next to the bed, the wardrobe with the multiple mirrors, the paintings she had bought at the Trevi fountain. Everything burned to ashes.

All that remained was the blackened brick shell of the now roofless house, a metal sign above the front gate that read 'Capri', and the tendrils of the bars blocking the now glassless windows.

Many of the neighbors, besides bars on the windows, had installed thin strands of wire to the glass surfaces that, when broken, triggered alarms. When infra-red alarms came to the market, they installed these too. With the innovation of motion detection, it too was added to the overall system.

Many years later, after the national political transition, all sophisticated attempts at the aesthetic arrangement of security devices were abandoned. These were replaced with the simplicity of a subscription to a QRASS, the Quick Response Armed Security Service, and a 12-foot wall of rudimentary brick or concrete walls topped with coils of barbed wire with access to the private entrances by remote controlled gates only.

This was not unlike the gates and fences that, besides the individual homes' security arrangements, several of the suburban districts surrounded entire neighborhoods with blocked and barricaded roads and singular entrances patrolled by armed guards.

But this was after the 'Maids Plot' was no longer called 'The Maids Plot' but called 'Crime' by many. By that time the Madam had returned to Africa, to her mother and brother.

...❧...

THE Madam had another button next to her bed, aside from the one she rang to call the servants to her bedroom. One ring, two rings, three rings.

The other button engaged a siren installed in the ceiling and unlike the momentary closure of the bell button that called the servants, this button remained engaged and the siren remained wailing, until the button was engaged once more, the contact released and the siren moaned to a halt.

Often when the Madam accidentally engaged the siren button instead of Lilian's button, the siren remained wailing for several minutes.

There were several reasons for this. The shock and surprise of hearing the sudden wailing banshee of the siren rather than the gentle note of Lilian's bell was shocking and caused momentary stupor until she finally recovered enough to stab at the button several times, muttering to herself as she did so.

Unfortunately, as she stabbed repeatedly at the button, the siren continued. It wasn't until, with continued repeated stabbings at the bell, she finally, in a combination of sheer persistent effort and luck, she hit the magical proportional combination of off and on that silenced the beast.

Some read the Madams' mistaken push of the button for the siren rather than that of the bell that called the servants as a sign of subliminal intent, or perhaps a subconscious desire, to engage or perhaps encourage, 'The Maids Plot' for some perverse, or unknown, or devious, or perhaps mistaken intention.

The Madam often pushed the siren button instead of the bell button that called the servants to her. When that occurred, the sound of the siren cascaded over the neighborhood walls, down to the surface of the water of the dam at the bottom of the road where it drowned in the water's lapping and the grunts and sighs of lovers in the back seat of their cars.

Back in the 'old' days, almost every night was filled with a plethora of wailing alarms triggered by pets, by unfaithful husbands, by drunken or drugged teenagers or simply by technical malfunctions of the equipment.

The false alarms became so frequent that the Madam finally just did not rely on the alarm anymore. Instead the silver foil on the glass, the thin wire and the bars on the windows, the two dogs, the three locks on the front door, the two locks on the back door, the locked iron gate across the passageway leading to the bedrooms, the locked glass door across the passageway leading to the children's bedroom, and the three servants at the back of the house, were sufficient deterrents.

All the men had a gun somewhere in the house as a final, close quarters resort. Many suffered various forms of arthritis or a variety of headaches because of sleeping on large metal lumps under their pillows. But the feeling of reaching under the pillow, the slight chill of touching the cold metal, made it worthwhile.

…~…

Chapter 27

The Maid's Plot

THE maid of each house is instructed to go to the house of the next-door neighbor and place poison in the water.

The 'Maid's Plot' initially spread among the Madam's during their daily morning chats on the telephone. Each time there was a ripple of abnormality to a daily domestic ritual, or sometimes on the occasion of sporadic civil unrest or the occasional overt riot, the 'Maid's Plot' would rear its head, creating ripples of suspicion that even the continued disappearance of the white sugar didn't allay.

The 'Maid's Plot' was based on the same arbitrary flip-flop of perception that governed most of the Madam's attitudes towards the servants. It presupposed the loyalty of the maids's to their respective Madams, Masters and their children.

Simultaneously, the presumption incorporated the recognition of a basic desire for vengeance against these same persons.

The validity of either of these two notions was open to question. Given the circumstance, each was true, either separately or combined.

Simultaneously, the presumption incorporated the recognition of a basic desire for vengeance against these same persons. The validity of either of these two notions was open to question. Given the appropriate circumstance, each was true, either separately or in combination.

However, in contradiction to both of these notions, these presumptions additionally denied the maids the ability to act on their own initiative, as it supposed an outside force instructing the maids. That same premise was then contradicted to some degree by crediting the Maids with the technical means to poison the water.

Was it that ribbed and sweating water jug that Lilian placed on the table each night that was going to be poisoned? Was it the glass of water the Madam placed next to her bedside in order to help the ingestion of her various pills? Was it the ice in the tray that remained in the freezer for years at a time? Was it the water that boiled so long on the stove together with the chicken's necks and feet?

...❧...

Chapter 28

The Dustbin Lid Plot

ON the day of the Revolution, all the dustbin lids would be missing from all the Madam's and Master's houses.

THE 'Dustbin Lid Plot' basis was an old tradition compared to the juvenile fifty-year heritage that formed the basis of the 'Maid's Plot'.

Dustbins, otherwise known as garbage cans, trash bins, trash cans or refuse containers in other English-speaking cultures, were usually kept in a small alley at the extreme rear of the house. In the Madam's house, the alley was closed off to the backyard by a high gate that was always locked and bolted. The dustbin boys, as they were known to the Madams and Masters, could access the bins without interfering with the household. They were entirely invisible to almost everyone until the pansela came at Christmas.

The Madam and her family had an inordinate subliminal fear of the dustbin boys. Perhaps their appearance promoted their fear to the very core.

Twice a week, the dustbin boys collected trash from the neighborhoods. A large truck lumbered along the side of the road at a constant five miles an hour, never stopping except for the occasional stop sign, which was ignored most often.

Running alongside the truck accompanied by shouts, whistles and horns, the dustbin boys darted into the alleyways. Without pausing, they lifted the large cans onto their padded shoulders and returned to the truck.

The truck, festooned with myriads of objects hanging from bits of wire and various types of string, rope and twine, like the dustbin boys themselves.

Anything reflective.

Anything that chimed, clanged, or banged against something else.

Any doll's head.

The dustbin boys should have been integrated readily by the Madams and Masters. They culled everything the dustbin boys wore or carried from the very households whose trash the Dustbin Boys emptied.

Their feet were bare, or in tattered tennis shoes, or dress shoes, or boots with no laces, or large and heavy sandals made from discarded tires with black and white geometric design cut out of the whitewall sections.

Apparently, it was the combination of men's and women's clothing, together with the electric wire and the hanging nylon brushes, that mostly drew the attention of the Madams and Masters.

That, and the neckties worn around sweaty necks with no shirt.

Neckties wrapped around their heads and cascading down their backs to waist level in a multicolored waterfall.

Dinner jackets worn with no shirt or tie.

Multi-colored strips of cloth tied to the end of a battered feather duster and held in one hand, arm raised to the sky.

Beaten whistles and plastic kazoos clenched between teeth and constantly blown in short staccato bursts.

On one shoulder, the wide, thick shoulder pad, held in place by two or three studded leather straps with large brass buckles that wrapped around their black and gleaming torsos like gladiators.

That, and the neckties worn around sweaty necks with no shirt.

These items instilled fear in the minds and hearts of the Madams and Masters.

The Madam or her family came into direct contact with the dustbin Boys only at Christmas when the dustbin boys performed the annual ritual of pansela.

The Christmas pansela ritual began with Lilian informing the Master that the dustbin boys were at the back gate for their pansela. The Master, gathering his serviette from his lap and tossing it on the dinner table, left the room and proceeded through the kitchen, down the back stairs, through the yard, past the mangy dog, to the back gate, where he threw back the bolt, undid the latch and pulled back the gate.

The sounds of shuffling bodies in the restricted space immediately halted. Ten faces peered at him in the narrow confines and silence of the dustbin alley.

The Master addressed the group sternly.

"Yes?"

No-one said a word besides the first man, who, after a pause, replied, "Pansela Baas?" in a low, quiet voice.

"Here", the Master said as he reached into the grimy coin pocket of his pants, grasped several coins, and distributed a single six penny coin into each of the outstretched pairs of hands that came forward and presented themselves to him.

"You can't all pick up here. You're too many. Maybe three, maybe four, this is skelem, what do you say hey boy!" the Master complained to no-one in particular as more and more pairs of hands presented themselves.

The dustbin boys just continued smiling and presenting themselves, some twice and one particular dustbin boy, three times, until finally, they retreated saying "Thank you my Baas, thank you my Baas."

The dustbin boys gathered at the junction of the Dustbin alley and the street, casually formed a circle and, introduced by the voice of the leader of the group, performed a short ceremonial dance.

It was only then, as the Master turned his back on the group to pull back the gate, throw the latch and back in the bolt, that the muscles in his stomach drew suddenly together in a pucker of subliminal fear as he noticed the lids were missing from the dustbins alongside him.

... ☙ ...

Chapter 29

The Mechanics of the Dustbin Lid Plot.

ON the day of the Revolution, all the dustbin lids would be missing from all the Madam's and Master's houses.

The conclusion that was drawn was the lids were being used as shields. This, of course, made complete sense to the Madams and Masters. Shields were the traditional defense instrument for these great warriors of past generations.

The dustbin boys, like the maids in the 'Maids Plot', credited them with the capacity to organize, in this case, a unified action of removing the garbage can lids from tens of thousands of homes in a swift coordinated action.

This would have left hundreds of thousands of dustbins open to the elements in the heat with all the accompanying hygienic hazards of flies, worms, and bugs. Perhaps most offensively, the acrid and pungent smell of the Masters' and Madams' own garbage would permeate their homes.

As a surreptitious signal of the upcoming revolution, this might have been a significant and perhaps appropriate sign, but practically it was lacking.

This would have left hundreds of thousands of dustbins open to the elements in the heat with all the accompanying hygienic hazards of flies, worms, and bugs. Perhaps most offensively, the acrid and pungent smell of the Masters' and Madams' own garbage would begin to permeate the homes.

There were two other inherent premises embedded in the idea of 'The Dustbin Lid Plot'.

They gave the dustbin boys no credit for having the practical insight to realize the futility of using dustbin lids as a defense against machine gun and rifle bullets.

The plot also held the premise of dependence. Without the Madams' and the Masters' dustbins, the dustbin lids would be unavailable and the Revolution would be a dismal failure.

The fantasy of 'The Dustbin Lid Plot' showed the Madams' and the Masters' prejudice for interpreting history in entirely European terms. The shields of the Knights of the Round Table were round and shiny, just like the dustbin lids and entirely unlike the oval cowhide shields the dustbin boy warriors carried in generations past.

Someone probably gleaned this prejudice from the Prince Valiant comic strip that was a regular back page feature of the Sunday newspaper section that the children so often fought over, without the benefit of any shields. The only shielding this family knew in history was the prayer book the teenager held in front of him while he stared wide-eyed at that red brick wall, waiting to be shot.

This rationalization, together with the usual presuppositions, prejudices, preconceptions and premonitions, kept the Madams, and the Masters terrified at the thought of the day when all the dustbin lids would disappear and they were defenseless without lids for the dustbins, a revolting smell throughout the house that would more than likely make the children vomit, and a revolution on their hands.

If 'The Dustbin Lid Plot' rumor hadn't died quickly, only to be resurrected as a distant memory to validate any new plot that arose out of the mire of innuendo, the burgeoning security industry would have been sure to have added yet another page of countermeasures to the voluminous list of self-protection gadgets in their catalogues.

The current Government was secretly involved in researching neutron weapons. These weapons were perfect for riot control and insurrections or revolutions of all sorts. Anyone within the limited radiation area is fatally irradiated. All structures, equipment and valuables, like rings or watches, remained intact.

Daniel Ellsberg, of Pentagon Papers fame, had revealed neutron research at a conference in Amsterdam in 1979, but the press overlooked it. The government was thankful for that, as well as the joint development with the American and Israeli governments.

"I will do anything for my country, even deal with Fascists!" said the Hero, the cousin of the Master, the concentration camp survivor.

...❧...

Chapter 30

The Revolution Arrives

MADAM: “Eeeeeeeeeeeeeeeeeeeeeeeeeeeeeeee”

She hadn’t screamed like that since her father’s death.

Maid: “Hauw Madam!”

Madam: “Oh my god, you gave me such a fright!”

She had imagined it being announced on the radio.

She had imagined it read by her husband from the evening paper.

She had imagined it happening in her bathroom.

She had imagined it happening in bed.

But not here, not now.

Not now.

Why this, why here, why now, why me?

The revolution had arrived.

Maid: "I am sorry Madam."

Madam: "What do you want, is it money?"

Maid: "I want a job Madam."

Madam: "Oh my God, Oh my God."

Lilian sat forward in the back seat of the vehicle, straining to hear and understand the Madam through the veil of her sobs and amphetamines.

"How much? I'll give you what I've got. You can come later when the Master comes home, at 6, he will have more for you then," said the Madam in-between gulping for breath, the heavy diamond ring on her finger chattering against the plastic of the steering wheel.

Maid: "I need a pass Madam, you said Thursday Madam."

"Thursday? Friday? Thursday…, was it Thursday?" the Madam thought to herself in a flood of conflicting associative thoughts and emotions.

"Oh…," she stammered plaintively, "I can't do that today, not today, I'm not ready, no ..., the car…, the children…, no Nanny..."

"But Madam said to come Thursday Madam."

"Is it really Thursday?"

"Yes Madam."

"Well…, let me see what I can do."

"Yes Madam."

With that, the Madam left Lilian sitting in the rear seat of the car where she remained until the Madam returned some twenty minutes later with fresh powder on her nose.

"Okay, Nanny."

"Yes Madam."

…❧…

Chapter 31

Inheritance

THE Madam's brother, Lennie, had five children, 3 of whom became known to the family as the 'professors', acknowledging that three of his children had gained doctorate degrees. His was good blood, as opposed to the, in his words, 'bad blood' that he considered flowed in the bodies of his younger sisters two adopted children, the sister who loved her adopted children dearly until she died of diabetes in middle age.

At the time of her death her brother told his brother-in-law he ought to disinherit his children, they were unworthy of any inheritance, they had caused the death of his sister with their antics and 'bad blood'. The brother-in-law kept his promise to his wife and looked after the children until his death in spite of their antics and the condemnations of his brother-in-law.

The Madam's brother was quite familiar with the management of inheritances. He had, after all, been the beneficiary of three large inheritances.

The first had occurred under somewhat complex circumstances. The Madam's grandmother had owned a farm in the old country. Her daughter, the Madam's mother, had met and married her husband at a young age and immigrated from Poland to what was Palestine at the time. There, together with several other members of her husbands family, they initially lived on the beach outside Jaffa, where the Madam was conceived.

Eventually the family moved to the town and with some success in the building trade, they built and lived in a house on what was now one of the main streets of Tel Aviv.

Then the depression of 1929 struck, extending well beyond the initial localized impact of the falling stock market speculations of Americans and impacting hundreds of millions of people around the globe.

The Madam's father was one of those millions.

While the other members of his related family were socialists or communists, he on the other hand, was a dedicated capitalist. When the depression struck and the bottom fell out of the local economy, his relatives were supported by the funds of the various unions of which they were members.

However, the Madams father, quite beyond the humility of taking what he considered was charity from the union, was without work. His set aside of cash and gold was soon depleted, at which point, in desperation, he, together with a number of his friends, decided to leave the 'promised land' and immigrate to Africa.

Neither the Madam nor her mother ever spoke of these events. They never mentioned their mode of transportation to Africa, nor the weather nor sights along the way, nor why they left Palestine or why they chose Africa rather than France or Argentina.

Even in later years, some 40 years later, when the Madam drove by the house that her father had built, she didn't make the slightest gesture or glance at the house as they passed, nor did she mention its existence to anyone in her family.

She and her mother both never mentioned the town of Skaryshev, nor the farm where her mother grew up, nor the market where her mother sold vegetables, nor the 7 other brothers and sisters in the family, nor the Albino aunt, nor the brother who was the editor of the newspaper of the Warsaw ghetto, nor the brother who was a shoemaker.

For the Madam the past started at high school and she remained faithful to that notion and her various classmates until she or they died.

It was only when the Madam's cousin, the socialist school principal who served on the panel that formulated words for modern inventions from the roots of the ancient language, who was so consistently kind, understanding and accepting all the years and even more so when she eventually went blind, it was only her recall that brought at least some of the details of the past to light, some confirmed by the Madam's mother on her death bed despite her sons insistence that she wouldn't remember anything, and that his mother only had two brothers.

Somehow in Africa, the Madam's parents started over, and somehow her father bought some land and built a furniture factory where he designed and produced various items of furniture.

Somehow his wife, the Madam's mother, with her retail experience in the market back in Skaryshev, opened a general and hardware store where she trained her teenage daughter in the mechanisms of buying and selling at a profit.

Somehow both enterprises were successful and somehow, within a short time, the family was in possession of a few factories, several development plots of land, several rental properties and a few blocks of apartments.

At this time the Madam met the Master.

He had seen her at a dance. He was dark and handsome, mysterious, already sexually experienced at a young age, initiated by an amorous and insistent older next-door neighbor according to him.

The Madam on the other hand radiated innocence and embarrassment at the attention he foisted on her. He spotted her across the room and literally swept her off her feet that night. She was entirely unused to such focused attention. She found herself both a little dizzy from the intoxication of his flirtation, as well as slightly afraid as she recalled many years later, adding, in response to being asked if she still loved him, "vi fefer in der noz!' (like pepper in the nose!)

But she had been infatuated by him at the time, despite the warnings from her brother, Lennie, who had been at the dance that night and witnessed the serenade before him. He was suspicious of the young man and even though he was some 3 years younger than she, a mere 15 years old, saw it as his duty to act against him, to defend her, to defend the family.

The Master had been employed as a warehouse assistant for a wholesaler of general goods when they were married. With little formal education and a lowly wage, he walked each Friday to his parents house, saving the penny that the bus ride cost, and contributed what he could from his weeks wages to his parents, or so he claimed.

At some point, somehow, he left that employment for some or another reason and is next known to be running a caning factory. When asked how he knew about caning the Master related that he knew nothing, that the 'coloreds' did the work while he ran the business.

Unacknowledged by the Master, the Master was actually set up in the caning business by his father-in-law and thus owed him a debt of thanks and perhaps a portion of the profit.

As described by many, his father-in law was a powerful personality, intolerant of others views or practices and unafraid to express or impose his views on anyone other than of his wife.

The father-in-law insisted the Master take in a partner of the father-in-laws choice to the factory. Apparently that partnership lasted a very short time. It's suspected that this partner was in fact the person the Madam referred to in later years as the victim of a violent physical attack by the Master, but that is pure speculation.

However, at a point, in the Master's retelling of events, he is somehow no longer associated with the caning factory and is unemployed or working at something unknown. Details of the disposition of the caning enterprise after his departure remain as mysterious as its initial formation.

The Master describes his next employment as being at the furniture factory of his father-in-law. He attains this employment because the father-in-law becomes sickly and is unable to work.

According to the Master, he, now in his early twenties, runs the furniture factory for about 9 months, initiating new designs and formulating more efficient production procedures and in general, running an organized and profitable enterprise, according to him.

Until one night, in the middle of the night, the Madam received a one sentence, three word telephone call from her brother Lennie.

"Daddy is dead."

She remembered this call in explicit detail her entire life though she never communicated her experience to anyone but her husband who was present when she answered the phone.

"She just screamed and screamed for the longest time", the Master said.

When her sister died some twenty years later she had not returned from the 'promised land' to attend the funeral. When her mother died, she hadn't called any of her children to inform them of her death. When her brother Lennie died a few years later, again she hadn't called any of her children to inform them of his death and refused to attend his funeral.

When these deaths occured, she had not attended the normal death and burial rituals of the religion, nor did she perform any of the annual memorials, the lighting of a candle, the dedication of a prayer, the visit to the grave, the placing of a stone. She remained forever mourning the death of her father privately, internally, until her own death released her from its hold. That was her ritual, that was her memorial.

The Master on the other hand, was quite familiar with the shock and isolation of death as both his parents had now passed away, as had his sister that day when she passed him carried by his father to the cemetery as his mother brought him home, wrapped in three thick shawls, newly born, according to him.

He had attended all the rituals of mourning for his father-in-law, reaching back to the heritage of his grandfather, a deeply religious man. He hadn't done this as a sign of any particular fondness towards his father-in-law, nor as any substitution for his wife's lack of involvement. He simply felt the need as a sense of duty, of obligation perhaps, to history, to culture, to spirit.

His grandfather would have had gone about the house unshaven, covering the mirrors with black cloth. He would have refrained from wearing leather shoes, a sign of luxury, but rather walked barefoot in the house, a sign of being humbled by loss. He would have eaten only round foods which recalled the cyclical nature of life. He would have sat low to the ground, on the floor or on cushions, a sign of being struck down by grief. He would have left the doors of the house unlocked so that visitors could enter without knocking or ringing the doorbell, distracting the mourners from their grief and causing them to act as hosts. He would have lit a large candle, the symbol of the divine spark that inhabited the body. He would have kept the candle burning for seven days, the seven days of creation, beginning to completion, the continuation of the cycle of life and death, the serpent eating its tail, the point at which the past flows into the future.

But now in this new country these rituals seemed superfluous unnecessary details which were distilled down to the ritual of candle lighting and seven days of mourning.

It was on that last evening of the seventh day of ritual mourning when Lennie, his brother-in law, walked up to him in the living room and asked, "Do you have the keys for the factory with you?"

"Yes," he replied.

"Well, hand them over," the seventeen year old said.

Surprised and somewhat confused by the sudden request, he innocently reached inside his jacket and handed over the bunch of keys to the boy waiting with his hand outstretched.

Accepting the keys, the boy turned on his heel and left the room to join his expectant mother in the adjoining room.

Before he exited the boy turned to the Master and said in a low voice, "You don't need to come in on Monday."

The Madam couldn't explain how she had responded to The Master returning home minus the factory keys, and minus a job.

Neither she nor the Master could explain how both of them continued to have a relationship with her brother for all the years until she left the Master. Neither of them could explain how her Mother, who was obviously complicit in her son's actions, had continued to visit her daughter every Sunday for lunch without fail, and where she engaged in lengthy conversations in Yiddish with her son-in-law to the complete exclusion of her daughter who consistently tried to interject comments into the conversation in English but that would quickly be dismissed by both of them, in Yiddish.

Neither of them could explain how following this dismissal by the Madam's brother, how the Master had come to be included initially in the running of the general goods store that his mother-in-law had established, groomed and given to the Madam to operate.

These conundrums remained unspoken and forever unresolved. They remained one of the perpetual undercurrents of the familial relationships between this family's mothers and daughters, sisters and brothers, between cousins and nephews and in-laws.

That day when the keys changed hands. No-one spoke of it, not that day, the day after or the week or the year after. This fundamental shift in the complex matrix of relationships was simply never mentioned.

But not forgotten.

...❧...

Thus Lenny, came to inherit the family's business assets, if not in the formal legal sense, then with the mantle of power and decision and the inherited priority of male lineage,

When his mother moved to an apartment some years later, he moved to his mothers house.

He claimed, and, once again with the complicity of his mother and the silent acceptance of his siblings, took possession of every stick of furniture, knife, plate and ornamentation, every object, memento and photograph of the old country.

It wasn't until after Madam's mothers death that it became clear the assets weren't legally transferred to his name until his mother had lain incapacitated in a less than luxurious long term care facility, placed there by her son, the same facility where she confirmed the existence of her 7 brothers and sisters.

This same facility was where, in her final days, propped up on several pillows and incapacitated, her son arrived and she signed the adjustment to her will that left everything to her son and nothing to either of his two sisters.

So complete was his assimilation of his parents business and their cultural and social assets that his older sister inherited only an inlaid plaque his father had made picturing a tent with a woman and a child greeting a returning father, and a simple clock that her mother had brought with from Skaryshev,

The clock had been kept in safe keeping by the albino Aunt Rivka for many years, until the Master, shortly after his separation from the Madam, had packaged the clock and sent it to his oldest son who never acknowledged its receipt. Perhaps it was lost in the mail or in the Master's son's hatred for him.

In fact the remaining assets were quite minimal when this late transfer occurred. According to the Master, Lennie had apparently already bankrupted the furniture factory and either sold or leveraged the real estate until all that remained were a few properties, including the building that housed the hardware store given by his mother to the Madam.

The Master over the years conducted a steady campaign to dismiss his wife as a business partner and gain complete control of the business. Finally, in a typical gesture, he renamed the hardware store with his own first name.

The Madam was finally relegated to dusting and arranging shelves in the store before she finally submitted and remained at home sleeping until noon in a haze of barbiturates while her husband continued to pay rent to his Mother-in-law via her son, his brother in law, the boy who had stood at the door that final night of *shiva* and demanded the return of the factory keys.

Lennie also controlled and according to the Master, within a short period, also bankrupted his wealthy mother in law's retail furniture store.

By the time the formal transfer of his mothers assets occurred, he also had access to his wife's substantial cash inheritance from her mother, as well as a substantial inheritance from a distant South American uncle that his wife had met only once, which included, besides a large cash amount, a valuable apartment in the 'promised' land.

...❧...

Chapter 32

The Niece

THE apartment had been managed by the Master on behalf of his brother and sister-in-law for a couple of years when these in-laws decided to send their youngest daughter to the 'promised land' and the safe keeping of his sister.

This was not uncommon practice for daughters of wealthy families. On many occasions, the daughters were paired with religiously compatible males who on their return to Africa were soon ensconced in 14 roomed mansions, with a speed boat and a share in the wife's fathers business and where they were often the most cruel to the employees and servants.

Lennie's daughter arrived at the Madam's apartment during the heat of the summer when the hot wind of the *hamsin* blew in from the deserts of Saudi Arabia. The shutters were drawn on the windows, as were the polyester curtains, a vain attempt at keeping the blistering heat out of the small third floor walk up apartment.

The air conditioner remained set in the window, unused since its delivery from the container of furniture they had delivered from Africa. Similarly the Venetian glass clown, together with the clear glass seal balancing a ball on its nose, remained on the flimsy pseudo Chinese shelf on the living room wall, the last remnants of their foreign tours arranged by Mendel, and of the bar in the house in Africa.

The young girl stayed for about 3 weeks until she came home rather late one night describing to the Madam that she had spent the evening with several other teenagers.

The Madam, gathering clues from the young girls description of the evenings events, immediately concluded that, on the beach that night, alone, the young girl had been taken advantage of by a boy, a man, an Arab, and would soon be pregnant if she didn't enforce some radical restrictions on the young girl.

In cowering fear of her brothers rage, overwhelmed by the notion of her responsibility for the possible consequences of the young girls vulnerability, in submission to her own wholly detailed construct of fantasized assault and surrender, she enforced a curfew that included not only fully supervised forays outside of the apartment, but additionally, at any other time, that is, when the Madam went to work each day, the young girl was locked, alone but secure in the apartment until her return.

...⁂...

Chapter 33

The Bus

IN the country she returned to, the country where the Madam was born on the beach, the mist of her own past lives had long faded away. She felt neither longing nor the urge to resurrect that life in Africa she had left 30 years before in the vain hope that perhaps she and the Master might start again but where she found herself even more bitter and resentful at the Master's infidelities and the failures of his dreams and his vain ambitions.

Her recollection of Lilian sitting in the back of the yellow Ford Zephyr, her scream, the maids' plot, the dustbin lids, Dinner and a Show, La Fontainebleau, had faded long ago.

Those years of darkened rooms, milked tea and Melba Toast merged with the memory of Lilian, Lilian who, over time, became her unacknowledged closest friend and dedicated caretaker.

Her journeys from one room to the other in the vacuous house were no longer. The apple cores and delicately peeled orange skin spirals were not the residue of a day's activity.

Going to work every day was one of the few notions she held onto that transgressed the borders between intuition and fact, that she doggedly maintained until she left for the airport that day, sobbing with desperation, and carrying less than her mother and father had left with, forty years earlier, headed once more for Africa.

The Master always dropped the Madam at the entrance to the building where she performed menial office tasks for a charitable organization that planted trees and then picked her up at the same spot some six hours later. They performed this ritual each and every day together with the several other rituals they performed each day, each and every day, without fail.

On the way to work, waiting at the traffic light to cross the main road, the Master always placed the gear lever of the tiny two-cylinder vehicle he drove after the Peugeot had expired, into the neutral position, between forward and reverse. The vehicle had only two gears, forward or reverse, and was basically a motorcycle with a cab.

With Lennie's daughter safely secured in the apartment, as usual the Madam and the Master sat silently in the vehicle, each lost in their own world, each lost to the other, each staring forward at the rear of a bus in front of them.

The driver of another bus, number 27, coming from the opposite direction on this busy street, as usual, as he did every day, except Saturdays, waved to the driver as he passed the number 14 waiting at the light in front of the Madam and Masters vehicle.

The bus company, a residue of the past socialist ideals of the then newly formed state, was employee owned and many of the drivers were long-time associates of other drivers or were perhaps relatives or neighbors of each other, or had served in the military together as well as being in the upper bracket of wage and benefit earners.

The 27 stopped as usual at the bus stop, some 50 yards down from the traffic light to allow passengers to alight and ascend. The 14, on seeing this in his large rear-view mirror and remembering his warm conversation with the 27 just yesterday, promptly put his bus into reverse and backed up to greet and chat once again, if only for a couple of minutes until the din of blaring horns and the protests of the passengers on both buses forced them to end the conversation, leaving with smiles, greetings and best wishes for each other's families.

The Master and the Madam still sat in their vehicle, simply numb and bewildered for those couple of minutes. Not much had changed. They both still sat silently in the vehicle. Both were still lost in their own worlds, each lost to the other, each staring forward.

Except, now they were some 200 yards back from where they had originally sat waiting for the light to change, but now the front of their vehicle was almost 12 inches smaller and hissing slightly but vehemently.

The reversing bus had hit the small vehicle with some force. Standing in neutral gear, without brakes or response from either the Master or the Madam, the vehicle had been propelled, freewheeling, in a perfectly straight line, until it stopped on its own accord, directly parallel to the cinema they never attended.

The two of them just sat there in the vehicle, staring forward, while the engine continued running for a short while until the water ran out of the crushed radiator and the engine overheated and shut down leaving only the glowing red light on the dashboard.

The driver of the number 14 came running up to the window of their vehicle and, on seeing that they were both apparently uninjured, proceeded to chastise the frozen faced Master through the closed window, for not honking his horn in warning as the bus backed up. This prompted some of the passengers of the 27, and then several from the 14, as well as a few passing pedestrians and then several of the backed-up drivers of other vehicles and the owner of the bicycle store on the corner, to enter the ensuing arguments.

The arguments continued throughout the various court proceedings that convened in the following months until finally, some 6 months later, the Master received a token compensation from the bus company equal to less than half the damage caused by the 2-ton bus. He decided to have the repaired vehicle painted a bright mustard yellow.

...~...

Chapter 34

Cum Si, Cum Sá

NOTHING came about as she expected it to be.

She had written on the back of a photograph of her youthful self at the beach with two friends; "Hoping this picture brings a smile to everyone who sees it."

When she was young, she expected life to happen just how she experienced it, she was so certain, so confident that those ideas, those hopes, those promises, would come about.

Now she found that her life had turned out not remotely related to her expectations, or those of others.

She hadn't expected that those gestures, those habits, those involuntary motions of hers that irritated or angered or nauseated others so often, in death, would be those gestures, those habits, those involuntary motions that would form such endeared and cherished memories of her.

The glance across the table at other's food.

The "Ah well."

The "Cum si, Cum Sa."

The furrows of stretch marks on her stomach.

The side-to-side motion of the jaw as she ground her teeth.

The "It doesn't matter."

The "It's not important."

The shake of the loose skin of her arm from the stroke induced tremor as she reached for yet another orange.

The smudge of blackheads that caked her nose.

The eyebrows that grew together.

The gnawing on the bone, on the skin, on the core, until there was nothing left but the stalk of the apple, the orange of the orange, the bone without the marrow.

The "Bye"

Gone now.

She never expected to die so suddenly.

She never expected to die so suddenly, and so alone.

She never expected to die so suddenly, and so alone, with her husband, her sons, her daughter, her grandchildren, her great grandchildren, so many thousands of miles away, so many unknown faces.

She never expected to die so suddenly, and so alone in that shabby infirmary with the stark and bare fluorescent light fixtures, the shiny paint on the walls and the polished concrete floor.

She never expected that she would be buried alone, that it would be a winters day with a cold wind blowing, that it would be September, that it would be 4 days after her seventy-ninth birthday, that her husband on hearing of her death would say repeatedly to Shaye, "My God, oh my God, what do we do now, what do we do now?'

She never expected that she would be buried in that cemetery where her mother, her father, her sister, and her brother lay, and never, that she would now lie so far away from them, in the new section, up on the hill, so alone under that African sky, where domes of lightning forked over miles of sky and thunder crashed and echoed for long seconds while in the summer heavy pellets of hail beat heavily on the ground above her and in winter the frost sheathed the tall grass so that it crackled as you walked through it.

She never expected that of her immediate family, only Lilian would be there at her graveside to bid her farewell.

She never expected to die so suddenly, and so alone.

...❧...

Chapter 35

Not Alone

THE irony of where she now lay wasn't clear until sometime later, after the shock of her death had passed and her tombstone was about to be raised. Here now in death, she was finally unconditionally admitted to the community that had passed such a critical eye on her and her family.

Around her lay the families of Shapiro, Cohen, Skutelsky, Weinstein and Weinberg. In row after row lay the descendants of Ber and Borochowitz, Campbell, Davis, Liebowitz, Fleishman, Milstein, Moscowitz, Sher and Levitt.

Spread over the granite boulder-strewn hills overlooking the open veldt were the graves of Gishen and Zeidel, Swartz and Lieberman, Alter and Eisenberg, Borochowitz and Goldberg, Gutman and Hamberger, Waksman, and Gitlin.

In section after section lay the community exiles from Poland and Russia, Germany and Austria. Some from Czechoslovakia and Transylvania but mainly from Latvia and Lithuania.

They had come from small towns on those outer edges of Eastern Europe, towns and villages like Jassa, Ponewes, Kovna, Shidlowo, Plunge, Kovna, Dushat, Taurage, Novyrad, Dvinsk, Kovna and Vitebsk.

They had spent some or most of their lives and often their hopes in towns like Bronkhorstspruit, Vereeniging, Kimberly, Messina, Mafeking, Nelspruit or Uitenhage.

Their children now lived in New York, Vancouver, Los Angeles, Brisbane, London, Tel Aviv, Toronto, or Baltimore.

Here were buried the families of Abrahamson and Abramowitz and Abrams and Aronson and Berkowitz and Berman and Bernstein and Bloch and Bloom and Blumberg and Brodie and Burger and Chait and Edelman and Epstein and Feinstein and Feldman and Fine and Finkelstein and Fisher and Frenkel and Friedland and Friedman and Furman and Gavronsky and Geffen and Gerber and Gersman and Getz and Glass and Gluckman and Goldblatt and Goldsmith and Goldstein and Golombek and Goodman and Gordon and Gross and Hershowitz and Herskowitz, and Hirsch and Hoffman and Horowitz and Hotz and Hurwitz and Hyman and Ichlov and Immerman and Isaackowitz and Isaacs and Isaacson and Israelowitz and Jacobs and Jacobson and Jaffe and Joffe and Kahn and Kantor and Kaplan and Katz and Katzen and Katzenberg and Klein and Klevansky and Kramer and Landau and Landsman and Lazarus and Levenson and Levin and Levy and Lipschitz and Magid and Mendelsohn and Meyerowitz and Miller and Myers and Nochomowitz and Rabinowitz and Rappaport and Rosenberg and Rosenthal and Ruben and Sacks and Schneider and Segal and Shein and Shuster and Silberman and Stein and Sussmann and Weiner and Weiss and Zuckerman.

Behind her to her right lay Lilie Markman and Evie Levin. Behind and to her left lay Freda Shapiro. Directly behind her lay Raya Chait. To her immediate left lay Iris Moskowitz.

In front of her, to the right, lay Mendel, and directly in front of her, a space for Nechama, wife of Mendel, arch-rival of the Madam.

This was the irony of her final acceptance to the community.

In this community, her sense of self lay in two spheres. For one, she lived vicariously through the lives of others.

Second, and perhaps more importantly, how others perceived her and her family was of the utmost importance. In this singular attribute, she shared a special unacknowledged intimacy with her husband.

She and her husband both spent much of their time and effort cultivating or adding to whatever premises, mistaken or otherwise, the community had of them or their family. They placed an inordinate importance on what could add, perpetuate, or embellish, any positive impression, factual or not, that the community, the friends, the neighbors, Nechama, had of them or their family.

It did not take actions on their part to create impressions or conclusions. They subjugated everything to superficial impression and perception first and foremost. Then and only then was that action evaluated in terms of its value to her or his own self expression foremost and never in consideration of theirThe pride in their children's achievements was something that was communicated to others, not to the children. The children, no matter what they achieved in pursuing their careers or their personal satisfaction or self-realization, were reminded they hadn't quite taken that step to would sufficiently meet the expected criteria, that would gain acceptance, that would win approval.

If a child's profession was a teacher, to all the neighbors and friends, they were a 'Professor!' If they were a social worker, they were a 'Psychologist!' or perhaps a 'Psychiatrist!' If they owned a few properties, they were in 'Real Estate!' If they were a doctor, they were a 'Surgeon!'

If the child was Mayor, they could be the Governor. If they were Governor, they could be President. If the child was a 'Manager', there was always some other relative, or neighbor, or friend, whose son, or daughter, nephew or niece, was the Director, or the Owner, or the CEO of some entity that made more money, or had more offices, or was city-wide, or national, or international.

Each time a child climbed the mountain of expectation, they realized on reaching the crest that there it was, another mountain to climb, with yet another crest. Cloaked in the amnesia of this expectation, they climbed that next mountain only to realize in the clarity of the thin air of high altitude, that there again, in the distance, was yet another mountain, with its accompanying toil towards the summit, with another crest, with another vista of the infinite peaks of expectation.

This was the circle of the spotlight on the need for recognition, that excluded individuality in the cause's pursuit, that transferred these values to each of the children, who fought vainly against the riptide of familial and social events and exclusions, in desperate efforts to surface as whole beings, free of the tyranny of their inheritance.

The children, like their parents, pursued their individual panoramas of intention with an extraordinary energy, only to find that often the passion of guilt destroyed that effort.

Or else, often they fell back, exhausted, glazed by the satiation of hollow pursuit, and, paralyzed by the realization of hopelessness, they lay panting at the altar of choices.

That is how the Master could say to the woman who replaced his wife after she left him, "If you leave me, I will kill you" with all the energy, love and passion of a killer.

How Shaye's attempts at untangling the threads of his past drew him to trust neither himself nor anyone else.

How the Madam was caught in the web of her own silent and desperate need for recognition and solace. When the envelope of diabetic stupor overwhelmed her, there was no-one there to hear that small and muffled intake of breath as she attempted to extricate herself and live another day.

... ❧ ...

Chapter 36

Mendel

MENDEL, who had traveled on the boat 'to France' with her husband's father all those years ago, lay directly in front of her.

Mendel, the Travel Agent, had booked them on those tours to return to Europe but never to the old country.

Mendel had booked the trip when they had toured the glass factory in Venice and bought hundreds of statuettes, vases and ornaments which they sold at a profit to their friends on their return keeping but a few, including the clown, the donkey pulling a cart, and the seal balancing the ball on its nose.

Mendel had booked the trip where they had seen the artist's painting in front of the Trevi Fountain and in the streets around the Sacre Coeur. They bought many of those hand painted oil paintings of scenes of vegetable and flower markets, sunsets on distant harbors, and a portrait of a clown with a tear in his eye, all of which they sold at a profit to their friends on their return, keeping but a few including the clown.

Mendel had booked the trip to America where they went to the top of the Empire State Building and bought the small copper replica that stood next to all the other souvenirs and mementos from their various trips without the children, to Mozambique, to Rhodesia, to South America, to Israel, to Europe, and where the Master had vainly attempted to find his Fathers brother or sister in Brooklyn.

The souvenirs of these trips stood in the glass showcase behind the bar next to the dining room with the bump under the carpet. The crystal from the chandelier in the Vatican, 2 glass swans from Italy, the book of matches from the Latin Quarter in Paris and Jack Dempsey's in New York, and the notebook of the dead Syrian soldier given to him by his cousin who had rescued his family from the Nazi concentration camp, never found the treasure under the tree, and still said, while dying from refusing to accept dialysis treatment, "I will do anything for my country, even deal with Fascists!"

Some of the children often visited this shrine of travel, peering into the glass cabinets with the locks on them, replaying the references the Master had made while the 8mm film projector flickered with snippets of their various vacations.

The parents never vacationed with the children. For three months at a time they left the children behind with the Madam's mother, who insisted on serving only half a chicken on Fridays, much to the surprise and consternation of Lilian.

They had once gone to the seaside with their children, ages three, six, and nine.

Some years later, on a Saturday afternoon, the Master dropped off the Madam and the three children for a weekend at the 'Wigwam Resort', a strange configuration of someone's fantasy of an American Indian encampment placed amongst the arid landscape of the Highveld. He picked them up again on Sunday afternoon.

That was the total of their Family Vacation experience.

Some years later, on a Saturday afternoon, the Master dropped off the Madam and the three children for a weekend at the 'Wigwam Resort', a strange configuration of someone's fantasy of an American Indian encampment placed amongst the arid landscape of the Highveld. He picked them up again on Sunday afternoon.

That was the sum total of their Family Vacation experience.

…❧…

Chapter 37

The Point of Freedom

THE moment she finally left him.

The moment she realized she had been holding onto the fear, the resentment, the notion, of feeling, of being, unworthy and unrecognized, and if she didn't act, her world would fall apart and she would have nothing, feel nothing, be nothing

The moment all considerations, options and fears fell apart, contradicted and made no sense anymore.

The moment her thoughts channeled into the sluice of her doubt and became a jumble of interconnected yet unrelated words and sentences, and she finally leapt from the realm of indecision to the domain of choice and responsibility.

The point of freedom became a reference, hollowed out of the ground of her sadness and desperation.

Even though she never experienced the moment again until the point of her death, it always acted as a reference for what she had achieved, rather than what was possible, a reminder, even then, of a defeat of sorts.

The other women, her contemporaries, the other women in the family, couldn't acknowledge this feat, this ability, this achievement, for to do so would have meant to acknowledge that most of them were in similar relationships with their spouses and they never plucked up the courage nor ever reached that plateau where the necessity of survival bubbles over, actions overwhelm thoughts, and freedom established as a marker.

...~...

Chapter 38

Shaye's Eulogy for his Mother

AT times of death, we have the opportunity of reflection, a moment to pause, a moment to consider, a moment to review.

I've been experiencing my mother's death for some years now.

My Mom wasn't a cheerful person, our family wasn't a happy family, that was obvious to everyone who knew us and eventually it was painfully obvious to us children.

But in our way, like so many families, we tried to make a better life, and we tried to be kind, generous, and considerate while doing so.

My Mom, my family, achieved or failed to lesser or greater degrees in that quest, but my Mom tried, often with great effort, often with loud noise and drama, and often with great heart and a certain grace and intelligence.

There were many who loved her, often in very silent ways. She gave me life, and in her death, she gave me life again.

My Mom's life started in a tent pitched on the beaches of Palestine and ended here on the Highveld of Africa. She loved James Hadley Chase novels, she loved Pitzah, and Melba toast with Redro fish paste. She loved to complain, she loved intricate family politics and intrigue. She loved her children, she loved Sylvia, and Hilda, and Lea. She loved her hair piled high in a beehive with lots of spray. She loved Doctors, and Pharmacists, and Pills, and Corsets, and Danish Herring, and Swiss Roll and Tea. She was a bright, inquisitive and mysterious person. She always had another layer, no matter how far you reached under the surface.

When she was young, she ran the hardware business her mother Sarah had passed on to her. I remember clearly her business acumen at the dinner table when she would say, “When someone comes in to buy some paint, ask them if they need a brush. If someone buys some screws, ask them if they need a screwdriver.”

My Mom loved to talk on the phone, as long as you called her. She stopped calling any of the children years ago. She would say in explanation she didn’t have your number, or the telephones didn’t work because it was Shabbat, or the phone broke, or the telephone exchange was closed because it was night, or the weekend, or a public holiday. There was always a reason. There were no blank spaces anywhere.

Except, in my last conversation with her, on the phone, after some time of her talking about wanting to see her great grandchildren, she suddenly interrupted our conversation mid-sentence and said to me, with long pauses in between;

“I just don’t know anymore ....,”

“I’m so confused ....,”

and then, after an even longer pause,

“I have to go now ...., I have to go ....”

And she was gone.

It was the last time I heard her voice.

But I keep on hearing her voice anyway.

My Mom said to me often as I was growing up;

"Oh, I might as well be dead."
In later years, she changed that to;
"Oh, I just wish it would end"
or
"Oh, when is it going to end?"
More recently, she would often say, with a sigh,
"Oh, I wish I were dead."
Well Ma, your wish is finally answered.
I hope above all else, your pain is over now, that you are at peace.
You tried so hard.

…~…

Chapter 39

The Suitcase

JACKSON helped to set fire to the suitcases that burned all the remaining belongings of the Madam. These were the suitcases that bore the stains of multiple layers of travel and abuse. These were the suitcases she had hurriedly packed when she finally limped out of the bathtub flushed with anger, naked and shivering from cold and exhaustion, embarrassed at the certainty of her husband's infidelity. These were the suitcases that bore the labels of trips to England that bore few fond memories. These were the suitcases that bore the meager contents of the cupboards already rifled many times by the aides at the retirement home. These were the suitcases that bore the good intentions and vehement denials and accusations of one brother against the other, of the sister against her brother, of one brother against the sister, of the sister against her uncle.

Eventually Shaye, who attended the unveiling of his mother's tombstone asked Jackson, his uncles garden boy, where he could build a fire, suggesting the rear of the house, behind the servants' quarters, where Jackson grew tomatoes, and corn, and pumpkins, and where his uncle and wife rarely ventured.

In their home language of Tsonga, Jackson's wife had asked Jackson, "Are those suitcases going to be burned? They are good ones. We can use them. Can we have them?"

Jackson asked Shaye, "Can we have the suitcases?" and when Shaye said, "No, I'm sorry, no", Jackson asked, "Can you maybe buy them?" and Shaye said, "No, I can't, I'm sorry, no," and Shaye gathered the sticks, wet from the previous days rain, and crumpled the newspaper that bore the previous day's news, laid the two suitcases on top of the pile, and, without opening the suitcases to view their contents, set a match to them.

Jackson and Shaye stood silently and watched as the flames grew and the smoke and smell rose in black puffs as the polyester dresses melted into black shiny puddles.

The flames, bright yellow and vehement orange rose high until they singed and then burned the leaves of the lemon tree that stretched in a canopy above the fire and the sour smell of plastic mixed with the pungent smell of lemons while the metal skeleton of the suitcase was progressively revealed.

Behind the fire, the corn stood high in silent witness, in unbending organic rectitude, an honor guard of forty-three with feathered headdresses, while the pumpkins slithered across the red dirt just short of the edge of the fire, and Jackson said, "Yes, it's finished now, it's finished now."

. . . ❧ . . .

Chapter 40

The New Dawn

THE mosaic fortress of coiled barbed wire plots and fences, the subdivisions of infrared beams and floodlights, the corridors of high walls and ornate compounds, where the hot summer air is punctuated by the staccato calls of millions of crickets, and the chorus of frogs, now violated by the progressively increasing howl of what starts with the singular bark of a lone dog at close proximity but soon grows in proportional increments to a cacophonous howling of multiple dogs, that increases steadily in volume and variety until it seems that the glass in the windows will implode, until a sudden "Hou op!" of the irate bleary eyed homeowner subjugates the central core of the maelstrom and the howling tapers off until there is once again only a solitary bark, but at a long distance, competing with an awakened mossie on a telephone wire, until that too is silent and the density of the African night takes over again with its vast hum easily confused with the blood pressure in your head, but that surmounts all of this attempt, this folly, this fear, until it too is punctuated by the irritating buzz of a mosquito circling erratically, louder and softer, louder and softer, focused like a high frequency sine wave in the center of your brain, and then, silent, like the guard dogs now, sucking blood until gorged and that voluminous silent hum of the African night dominates everything once again.

There is never silence in Africa.

...❧...

BOOK II

THE CHILDREN

BOOK II

PART I

Chapter 1

The Daughter (1)

THE eldest child, the daughter Rebecca, married Bennie, a young man from a small town who didn't smoke or drink.

Since her sixteenth birthday, she had adopted her husband as a bulwark against the tide of her history, as her threshold to another reality, as a concept of a different way of being.

When she married, she moved to the hometown of her husband, some six hundred miles away, despite the desperate efforts of her parents to keep her in the local area by offering her their home, lock, stock and barrel, furniture, crockery and servants included.

In that small parochial town close to her husband's birthplace, she began ingratiating herself to her husband's parents and defending herself against the thrusts and parries of the three other daughters-in-laws who also lived in the town and who were similarly competing for various acknowledgements from the parents-in-law, monetarily and otherwise.

Her attempts at acceptance by her husband's family, particularly her mother-in-law, were colored by the stain of her own family's imprint on her ability to differentiate between genetic allegiance, competition with the other 3 daughters-in-laws, and her own basic savage instincts inherited from her father.

What was never acknowledged by either the Madam or Rebecca and remained a subtext to their relationship until the Madam died, was Rebecca's inextricably being drawn to doing better than the other daughters-in-law of her husband's family. In the furtherance of that quest, she eventually virtually disowned her mother despite her teenage role as the family go between, and her subsequent 'PhD.' in Social Work.

This competition with the other 3 women combined with an overarching need for acceptance and recognition would eventually destroy her relationship with her youngest brother Shaye, her mother, and ten years of her relationship with her father, and similarly for some lengthy periods with Nathan, her other younger brother.

Rebecca had refused to allow her mother to attend the birth of her first child, her mother's first grandchild. The Madam, in a typical effort at reconciling her inner self with her outer experience, never forgot nor forgave Rebecca, and unfortunately, neither her grandchildren for this rejection.

Her own awkwardness at motherhood was only amplified by her inability to establish a relationship with her grandchildren that ventured no further than the precursory peck on the cheek on greeting or leaving them, or the millionaire son-in-law's constant attempts to prompt his in-laws to establish a fund to pay for his children's college education.

The Master and the Madam continued to visit Rebecca for an increasingly strained two-week visit once a year until, after several years, they suggested moving to the same town in some fantastical hypothetical dream of solidifying the myth of happy grandparents.

An extended period of plans and negotiations for apartments and green cards ensued until Rebecca informed the Madam that she and her children would be not obliged to visit their grandparents every Friday night. The children would visit but "only if they wanted to".

That put paid to the Madam and the Master's plans and they returned to their isolation without establishing a fund for their only grandchildren's college education and with one more notch of resentment and disappointment on their staff of regrets.

Rebecca, immigrated to the United States, running in fear of the rising tide of what she perceived as the oncoming revolution in Africa.

To Rebecca and Bennie's delight, already qualified as a social worker in Africa, Rebecca discovered that in the United States she could legitimately practice as a psychology therapist.

Rebecca practiced for a short period as an employee of a local community center until she gathered enough information to practice as an independent therapist.

She soon discovered that, using the model of Bennie's dental practice, she could expand her practice and increase her profit by hiring other therapists and keeping a percentage of their fee. She also discovered she required a Ph.D. Degree in order to qualify for the various insurance claims her practice would make.

Rebecca received her Ph.D. Degree by correspondence from an obscure college in California, complaining when the hour-long final exam ran up her long-distance phone bill.

With her doctorate in hand, she opened an independent social work practice. Together with the other therapist employees, she saw clients in her basement and then, as the practice grew, she made an addition to the house that functioned as both office and her exercise room.

Rebecca practiced in this manner, until the neighborhood committee, frustrated by the constant stream of cars and the resulting limited parking in this upper-class townhouse community, forced her to move and find legitimate office accommodations.

Under the strain of competing with her sisters-in-laws and the purchase of a second residence on a riverfront complete with jet skis, boats and the luxury vehicles to tow them, Rebecca apparently pleaded poverty to her father and had him pay for furniture for her new office.

The Master agreed even though several years before he had removed her name from his bank account as a co-signatory saying bitterly, "She's been helping herself to the money without asking or telling me!"

…❧…

Chapter 2

The Rings

REBECCA acted in a similar manner when, on another visit, the Madam had taken off her large diamond engagement ring and presented it to Rebecca in a grandiose gesture of mother to daughter, saying “I want you to enjoy it while I’m alive, not when I’m dead”.

As soon as the Madam departed, Rebecca had the ring taken apart and reset, using the individual diamonds for a pair of earrings, a necklace, and a brooch.

Rebecca claimed it was within her right to do with the gift as she pleased. Rebecca rationalized that if the Madam wanted her to enjoy the gift, she, Rebecca, could enjoy the gift just as she saw fit. According to Rebecca, if her actions hurt or offended, that was unfortunate but the Madam was imposing herself on her independence and self-determination.

The Master and the Madam were both devastated by these actions of Rebecca, both towards them, and to the sanctity of what they considered a family heirloom. It remained a constant bone of contention for the Madam until her death, and to the Master, until he perverted the ring to the intentions of his own self-aggrandizement.

It was some years later, unprompted by anyone, the Master pointed out to Rebecca it was unfair to the other two children for her to have received these gifts of large value besides everything else she received from them over the years.

To this she agreed. She would pay each of her siblings one third of the jewelry's value.

There was, however, a caveat, a condition for the terms of the transaction.

She would pay each of her siblings one third of the amount calculated on the price the Master had paid for the stolen diamonds he had bought from Mr. Kajee, some 40 or more years before, not the actual or current value of her cache.

...❧...

THE Master, now separated from the Madam, after being estranged from his daughter for many years, on reconciliation with her, on one particular visit, searched through his daughters' teenage children's drawers while the others were away.

In one grandchild's drawer he discovered the discarded setting of the wedding ring he had given the Madam many years ago, and which the Madam had passed on to Rebecca as a family heirloom.

He re-appropriated the discarded ring and held onto it secretly for several years until one year, on a visit to Shaye, he proudly displayed it again, less than a year after the Madam's death.

...❧...

Sitting at a diner over breakfast, he ordered his new companion, the Dutch Lady, a gentle woman, a survivor of the Holocaust, to "show him, show him".

With insistent elbowing from him, she obediently turned over her hand, which had been resting on the tabletop, and reached forward towards Shaye.

As the Dutch lady posed with her hand above the table, Shaye stared at it in confusion.

With great pride the Master said, "That's Mommy's ring. You know I found it. Thrown into a drawer in Julie's room. Just like that, just thrown into a drawer. You remember the story of the ring. How your sister changed it. I had it set. A zircon, but that doesn't matter. What do you think, huh? What do you think, huh?"

Shaye, initially numb, mumbled an indistinct and unintelligible reply to which no-one responded.

He slid out of the dining booth clutching the bill for their meal and left the waitress an extraordinarily large gratuity, apologizing for the crumpled and slightly soggy bill he handed her

. . . ❧ . . .

IT wasn't until several months later, when, together with Shaye receiving the forwarded letters and packages from the Man from California, Shaye pondered a much more essential question. A question that would compound both fear, growing suspicion and understanding, enveloped in one delicate gauze cocoon.

Why was the Master secretly going through the private drawers of his twelve-year-old granddaughter?

In this light, the vulgarity of re-appropriating the ring for his new girlfriend paled in comparison.

The steady and progressive disintegration of the Master as a Father figure, as the Hero stabbed just above his appendix by the bayonet of the German soldier, as the Holder of the mysterious diary of the dead Arab soldier, as the popular Victim thrown into the river, the Guardian of the pack of non-filter Camels, the Magician of the flickering light, found yet another foothold.

...~...

ON another occasion, prior to her reconciliation with her father, Rebecca, via a proxy, had sent several of the Masters mementos in her possession to Shaye saying, “I don’t want to be reminded of him.”

Several years later, the Master enquired of her where these mementos were, to which the Master reported, she replied, “Shaye has them”, failing to state she had sent them to Shaye or why she had given them over to him.

This was standard family practice, conclusions, or presumptions by omission. Her father practiced this with the chips made by Etti, Rebecca by leaving out parts of a sentence, allowing the listener to draw their conclusion, which she would correct only if the subsequent conclusion didn’t paint her in a positive light.

Rebecca practiced variations in several interviews with the press.

In one interview, in a blatant confusion of guilt and hypocrisy, she attempted to proclaim herself a Liberal and described her intolerance for the fascist government and the lifestyles of her remaining family in Africa.

This was greeted by these families with much chagrin, consternation and condemnation plus a fair amount of cynical hilarity from those family members who knew her better.

To them the notion of her as a liberal, concerned for the rights of the black population, was so completely in opposition to her lived reality, they laughed uproariously and passed it over as a weak attempt at finding acceptance in the United States or else a sorely late and impotent attempt at reconciling her past with her future, or her guilt with her greed.

Several years later, again in the public forum of the Press she extolled Family Values, the healing nature of forgiveness, and her ability to give her father back his ‘lost family’ as an 85th birthday present.

However, Rebecca held onto the gold cake lifter that Shaye had guarded for so many years, packing it into his backpack and carrying it, through various meanderings across the continent of Europe, much like his grandfather.

The Master had approached Shaye one day and asked him to give over the cake lifter to Rebecca, saying to him, "she's collecting silver".

Maybe the lifter didn't remind her of her father. Perhaps it was simply gold to her, of no sentimental value. Perhaps, to her, it was simply an aesthetic object that lay in a silk box with some curious hand-written script in a foreign language on the inside to be placed on the glass shelf together with the other silver knick knacks she had collected. For her, family blood was as thick as a dollar bill.

She sent Shaye all the Masters memento's but not the heavy white gold cake lifter.

Yet, this was the cake lifter that was given to the Master's mother on the occasion of her wedding, by her sister, the eggs and hides merchant who were carted off to Siberia and whose husband had shouted to the young boy hero-to-be, "the money is under the tree," as the train left the station.

This was the cake lifter that was the sole residual material object that remained of the Masters family from the old country, besides the discarded photographs of Sholom and the rest of the family on the basement floor on the other side of the Irish Green room.

...~...

Chapter 3

The Basement

THE basement of Rebecca's house was the crucible for several critical events in the lives of this family.

The Master had fits of private rage at the granddaughters 'canoodling'. He couldn't stand seeing his grandchildren making out with their various boyfriends in the basement.

He raged at the indifference to his family heritage that Rebecca displayed by not looking after the number of family photographs he had passed onto her many years before.

He left them to her care in the 45 gallon barrels that stood in her garage in Africa, now pilfered by various people and simply abandoned, aside from a few scraps shipped to the United States in deference to some vague familial allegiance that Rebecca would later claim as her quest to restore her father's family to him.

The Madam ordered a container full of new furniture, appliances, crockery, cutlery, soap, and toilet paper for their new life in the old country.

The Master packed barrels and shipped them to Rebecca, together with their furniture and belongings from their home, amassed over some 40 years.

It was an eclectic collection, as most family accumulations are.

The Imbuia sets, the mahogany dining room set with the Chinese motif on the drawer fronts, the lounge chairs and settee that were named the Lesli, the Esti and the Baylah in the factory his father-in-law established, the remainders of the Venetian glass they had brought back from Italy and sold to their friends, the small mementos from their trips abroad, the Eiffel tower key chain, the ashtray stolen from the Hilton Hotel in Istanbul, the glass chandelier segment from the floor of the Vatican, the matchbook cover from Jack Dempsey's, the photographs of his family, his father, his mother, the photographs of his grandfather, the man he called Yona but who was actually named Sholom, that lay on the floor of the basement until he rescued them by asking his youngest son to take them away.

Almost all gone, sold or abandoned by Rebecca in her quest for Modernity and competition with her sisters-in-law. The china, the Passover crockery, the Venetian blown glass candlesticks, all gone now, except for the few photographs on the floor of the basement, the gold cake lifter, the gold and the diamonds.

...❧...

Chapter 4

The Daughter (2)

ONE year, Rebecca's parents had given her a sum of money to renovate her basement so that they might have better accommodations for their annual visits.

They returned the following year after receiving several enthusiastic correspondences from Rebecca describing the ongoing renovations. On their arrival, they found Rebecca had indeed renovated the basement.

At the picture window end of the basement, Rebecca had installed a disco dance floor with several sets of embedded blinking lights. The rest of the voluminous room contained a pool table and several other entertainments, a pin-ball machine, Fusbal, several couches and bean filled cushions.

In the rear quarter section of the basement, Rebecca installed a bathroom and adjoining that, a windowless room that accommodated a double bed, a desk, and a file cabinet, in all occupying about 1/8th of the basement.

This Irish Green, windowless, dark and musty area, just on the other side of the discarded family photographs on the floor, was the designated accommodation for her parents during their visits to her.

However, the windowless space at the rear of the basement also served as the office for Rebecca and her employees' therapy sessions.

Often during her parents' visits, the Master and the Madam would have to scramble to vacate the room for the visiting clients.

The therapists would also have to scramble to make up the bed and throw the discarded underwear and pungent polyester clothes into the nearest closet before their clients entered.

The therapy group specialized in behavior modification, and they did so in a manner not dissimilar to the local mechanic down the street that specializes in 'All Foreign Makes' or how Nathan would conduct his late career in London many years later.

Rebecca had a tall cabinet for 'action' sheets, each shelf labeled with titles like - Divorce, Separation, Death etc. which she handed out to the various clients.

As a therapist, Rebecca was convinced behavior modification was the cure-all for all abhorrent or deviant behaviors and that any depression therapy that didn't cure the client in 5 to 10 sessions was invalid.

She took on clients for Bereavement Counseling, Divorce Mediation, Couple Counseling, Anxiety, Depression, Anger Management etc. etc. She was the Jiffy Lube of Psychology Therapy practice,

Often she made 'charitable' gestures to those clients who could not afford ongoing therapy with her, or were more desperate or financially unable or uninsured. She had her house painted or cleaned by her clients. She had clients do her secretarial tasks, her correspondence, accounting, and billing. Several clients exchanged artworks in return for therapy. Another client composed and performed a custom song for her daughter's bat- mitzvah. Others did her family's laundry. All in return for 40 minutes of therapy with her.

This exploitation of her clients was directly contrary to the ethical standards of the State Board of Social Workers, but no-one made a claim against her for this abuse, while she made several claims against her clients for outstanding debts.

... ❧ ...

Chapter 5

Who She Was

REBECCA swaddled her father in the toxic cloak of inherited vanity, vehemence and vengeance that she knew only too well as a victim of his attacks herself and that she now transferred to Shaye with the same dogged determination she shared with her siblings.

This transference, the same transference that victims of sexual abuse, the victims of torture and of war, child victims of adults, who, given the opportunity, choice are drawn, again and again, to replicating, inflicting, perpetuating, the same suffering on others as if this would somehow drain the boil of their victimization, heal a bleeding wound that was already a scar.

How Rebecca would disinherit herself from her family at the young age of sixteen and mount the genealogy of her husband from the little town to the south.

How she could respond to her estrangement with Shaye as the result of a sour joint real estate venture with a letter that read:

"Yes, even though I/we knew you were upset, I went ahead, disregarding your point of view. Yes, I knew then, that disregarding your point of view would hurt you and make you angry with me – and I still continued on my path (I knew this would be the consequence, and was willing to accept this consequence) But at that time, and now looking back, I would have chosen a different path, if I knew that the cost was to lose you as a brother."

…❧…

Chapter 6

The Son-In-Law

BENNIE was everything the Madam and Master had wished for from their two sons but which they both failed to deliver. He was an aggressive personality, his primary interest being to accumulate wealth at all costs, no partner, family or friend excepted.

He always saw opportunities for profit and often pursued those opportunities, but in a small-town sort of way, in a low budget sort of way, in an opportunist sort of way, in an uneducated populist sort of way.

He was an unbridled capitalist entrepreneur who rode the mount of whims and then discarded them just as easily as he gained them.

While studying at dental school, he sold cufflinks to his classmates made of scraps of mosaic tile samples from his fathers-in-law's hardware store.

When his classmates were required to engrave their dental instruments with their names, he purchased an engraving machine and scratched their names onto the instruments at a discounted price.

It was no mistake of circumstance that he exhibited all the qualities of a second-hand car salesman.

When the son-in-law graduated after failing his dental exams multiple times, to where there was the very distinct possibility that he would be excluded from the profession entirely, in England, where he went for a year to practice dentistry, he sold cars to other dentists coming over for their own ritual visit to England.

On his return to Africa, he attended some evening classes in pottery for a few weeks. When he no longer saw the value in paying the school for the use of the wheel and kiln, he decided he could have unlimited use of a wheel and kiln as well as bring in additional income by conducting pottery classes of his own in the basement of his home.

When he became enchanted with English sheep dogs, upon finding out the price of the pedigree breed, he decided he could get a dog for free and make a profit by breeding the dog in a fenced in area next to the swimming pool at the bottom of his garden. His various servants cleaned up both the swimming pool and the dog excrement.

In fear of the perceived oncoming revolution, he and his family left Africa and immigrated to America, where he continued this litany of ventures.

His first venture in America was a partnership with his cousin, Warren, in a dental laboratory in the basement of Warren's house while he waited to be accepted for a License to Practice in that State.

While that initial venture had limited success, a later venture expanded into a full and successful dental practice in partnership with Warren.

With several dentists working in the practice, he continued to partner with Warren in a cardboard container factory, then an audio-visual production company, and then a local newspaper they hoped to transform into the ever popular 'Swop Column' he and his wife poured over for hours in bed back in Africa.

When all those ventures failed, he partnered again with Warren to bring carpets and copper plaques illustrating wild animals and naked breasts from Africa, which they attempted to sell in temporary space in a defunct mall.

When that failed, again with Warren, he ventured into attempting to sell advertising on parking meters and trash cans.

As the first location, the City allowed a trial run in the center of downtown. Unfortunately, the exclusive area was also a National Historic Preservation District. Neighborhood opposition doomed the attempt in short order.

Warren was familiar with advertising. He and Bennie had been the first in the state to take advantage of the newly instituted regulation by the board of dental practitioners that allowed dentists to advertise.

Warren ran several successful advertising campaigns offering free dental examinations, two for one x-rays, discounted dental cleanings, free toothbrushes, acceptance of any and every insurance plan, all much to the chagrin and disdain of the established dental practitioners.

He shipped boxes of several thousand fliers in plain, hand addressed envelopes to England, where they were mailed back to the United States with British stamps.

Warren spent every day for some years coordinating the advertising campaigns for the dental office, often to the detriment of his other business ventures, and his marriage.

But Bennie dismissed those efforts of his partner when the partnership failed. Much in the same way he dismissed the efforts of Shaye whom he had partnered with in a real estate venture.

...~...

Chapter 7

The Nation, the Tickey and the Son-in-Law

"WE are a small but brave nation, and we shall overcome them."

It was the Six Day War, 5th June, 1967.

The homeland was at war.

Children listened over the radio to the progress of the sudden war against their cousins, uncles, aunts, relatives and friends of all kinds.

The mythology of David facing Goliath was re-enacted.

Young men volunteered and flew off to help in the defense of the Promised Land, only to find it was all over on their arrival.

The community gathered to support the State, their cousins, uncles, aunts, their relatives.

... a coin smaller than a thumbnail, thin as a wafer ...

An auction to benefit the homeland was proposed and organized. Men pledged thousands of pounds, of which only a small percentage was ever met.

Many women, gathering at tea parties, overwhelmed by their emotions, put forward grand gestures toward their social status and stripped diamond and gold rings from their fingers, gold, diamonds and pearls from their ears, gold, diamonds and pearls, and emeralds from their necks, and dropped them in the bowl as it was passed around.

Another donor at another gathering donated a tickey, (three pennies or two and a half cents), a coin smaller than a thumbnail, thin as a wafer, but nothing to sniff at. This was no ordinary tickey. This was a 1931 tickey, an extremely rare coin worth a substantial amount, once again donated by the anonymous donor in an emotional moment of blind generosity towards the beleaguered Homeland.

Bennie attended the auction, hoping, like many other attendees, to gather a bargain from this bonanza of emotional giving. With some experience in coin collecting, (his father-in-law and Shaye had collected coins and started him into the details of collecting), quite aware of the value of the rare coin, the son-in-law bid for the 1931 ticke. To his surprise ,and the glowing adoration of Rebecca, he won the 1931 tickey at not nearly the collector value.

The next day, the Master received a call from the Chairman of the organization that held the auction. They realized they had inadvertently sold the 1931 tickey without reserve. They were requesting, considering the cause supported by the auction, the coin be returned.

Bennie refused.

Who he was, was clearly apparent that day and should have been a clear warning of what was to come.

Instead, his luck and good fortune was jealously admired by his in-laws as inherent and highly valued abilities that would benefit Rachel.

The other family members, the Nation, the Promised Land, be damned. This was money! This was a bargain!

...~...

BOOK II

PART II

THE ELDER SON

Chapter 1

The Elder Son

THE middle child, the elder son, Nathan, realized that he was gay while still very young. In a neo-fascist, national socialist environment, it proved difficult to reveal his sexual identity, as well as pry himself from the toxicity of the Master's often silent assaults, he left his parents, his family, and the country at the first opportunity.

His mother said he was gay because he caught his testicles in his crib one day.

His father expressed nothing but hatred and disappointment in him.

His penchant for young Arab men in later years was a typical 'in your face' gesture towards the Master.

Not yet in his twenties, Nathan established himself in London, England, where he developed a Queen's English accent in very short order.

After several years of apprenticeship and failed relationships, he became a hairdresser much to the distress of his varicose veins, part of his psyche, and his parents.

Besides developing a Queens' English accent, he was also quite adept at embellishing his resume, career, and his subsequent social standing.

After several years of being on the dole and failed attempts at making a living producing less than attractive handmade greeting cards, not having any degrees or qualifications to enter a university or college, he received a certificate in psychiatric nursing.

With that singular qualification, he and a partner set up a commercial venture that provided certification for various mental health worker skills by mail, via internet or fax, in weekend sessions or in afternoon lectures at seedy hotels or at 'offices' in a seedy part of London.

He '*re-trained as a Counselor*', but failed to mention, and least of all to mention in his public literature, where he studied, or what certificate or degree he had received.

Presumably revitalized by his '*re-training*', and '*qualification*', he apparently then '*developed a large purpose-built, open access, counseling center*', which somehow didn't have a specific address to reference.

In the literature that promoted this business, the six months spent studying graphic design at the Art School in Cape Town, was spent as an apprentice hairdresser while continuing to accept the money sent to him by his parents for his Art school education. His resume described this period as '*a first career in Art and Design*'.

His promotional literature stated that he later '*developed his counseling skills using art as a therapeutic tool*' but gave no information on how, or where, he studied these skills, or what skills these were.

His many years standing scrubbing saboraic scalps, cutting hair and listening to the complaints of customers, his promotional material described as '*experience in the fashion industry*'.

The many many years he was on the dole and begging his mother for money for yet another home 'so he could feel secure', his promotional material covered that era as, '*working for many years in the voluntary sector*'.

He continued to live in England for many years, where his accent become coarse and hollow as his age and weight increased, until he was bloated almost beyond the point of recognition, and where he continued to hate his father and Shaye with vicarious and vicious vehemence salted with more than a touch of vindictiveness.

Nathan eventually landed, ostensibly penniless, in a bed-sitter apparently losing almost everything he had gained financially on an adventure in Turkey. According to him, the Turkish mafia successfully ousted him from ownership of all things, a burger restaurant whereupon he had to flee back to England where he pleaded victimization in a televised appeal to his Councilperson. The Turkish authorities, on the other hand, claimed he had committed various tax evasions.

...❧...

BUT then, presumption, rumor and innuendo can color both fact and fiction. Those gaps between the inferred, and the implied, 'The Chips' and the 'Maker of Tasty Chips' were moments where the desperate need for recognition, the simple acknowledgement of validity, sometimes takes desperate measures.

Those moments were denied to others in Nathan's campaign against anything related to the Master, including Shaye, his younger brother, who shared a room with him for fifteen years, both in virtual silence.

Nathans ultimate victory over his father was, of all the children, he benefited the most financially from his father. Two flats in London and the money gained from their secret sale disappeared, unrepaid, while he begged his mother for yet another apartment.

When the Master insisted the 3rd apartment be in the Masters' name as a precaution against yet another disappearance of the money and perhaps a further request for yet another apartment in the future, Nathan refused the condition saying, "If it's not in my name, I don't want it."

...❧...

A Consequence of Lust

"I regret the moment that I conceived him."
Master referring to Nathan.

Nathan

Chapter 2

Happy Birthday

A Letter from Nathan to his Father

MY *Mother signed a will leaving her estate in equal shares to her children. She did this believing that when she authorized the sale of her jointly owned flat in Israel, her legal entitlement would be held independently. My Mother was not greedy and as far as I am aware, she made no demands of you to share assets stashed away and secreted by yourself over the years.*

I now am informed that my Mother died with some underwear and a few dresses as her estate. The explanation I have been given is that she had had her money "in advance." It is clear that when my mother signed her will it was known to you that in fact there was nothing to leave and that she had been defrauded out of her share. My guess is that you would see this as just and miss the fraudulent and criminal nature of what you have done.

Gosh if ever there was an example of moral corruption, this is it!

I also understand that you plan on being at her unveiling. I didn't think that even you could be so hypocritical. I assure you that my Mother does not wish you to visit her grave. She didn't want to hear your name let alone have you near her and whilst I could not prevent your abusive behavior to her (and at least two of your children) in the past, I can stop you now!

As my mother's older son I will be personally arranging a memorial to her according to her expressed wishes and I will be meeting the expenditure.

As far as this $50,000 is concerned, I wish to have nothing to do with this (or any other) corrupt money. The fact that you are "prepared" to honor her wishes is irrelevant. My Mother was defrauded out of her legal entitlement and this money should have been in her keep and not yours to make decisions about.

I understand that you believe in God and a life hereafter. May God forgive you as my mother would not have done so for this final act of abuse.

...❧...

ON first observation, Nathan's words and promises were not shown to be in direct contrast to his actions. There is no indication his expression of morality and defense of his mother were entirely false, nothing but a posture and everything he could muster in revenge at the time.

His words showed nothing of the hollow echo of his vessel of vanity.

They showed nothing of the piercing wail of the tumultuous voices that were born from such pain, that overwhelmed him, that ground away at his teeth even while asleep, that couldn't be washed away with multiple showers or baths, that permeated the cloth of his pretension despite the layers of deodorant, after-shave and the washing of his hands, multiple times.

That still remained, even though all these years, he still constantly rubbed the inside of the palms of his hands until they were bright pink and raw.

He never did arrange and pay for his gallantly proposed memorial to her.

He never visited his mothers grave.

He cashed the $50,000 cheque without so much as a distant murmur.

...❧...

Chapter 3

Shaye's Dream

I dream of kidnapping him. Waiting in an alley and grabbing him as he walks past, having just left his office. I dream of holding him in a hotel room, bound to a chair. I see his bloated red face on its background of pasty grey, the spittle dripping from his mouth, his eyes narrow. He is talking constantly, spilling anger and vehemence. He is straining against the ropes, not in any attempt to escape, but bulging like a hysterical Michelin Man, spewing hate towards me.

There is that moment, before I can edge closer, when I realize he is helpless in his tirade, that I am no longer paralyzed, frozen in the moment that I always translated as simply observing, but I now know as transfixed fear.

He doesn't have any power. I have the power now. I have the power to inflict pain on him.

But I want to inflict pain on him directly. I want him to know that the pain he is experiencing is coming directly from me, not confused with any other source, directly from me. Not from a knife or a blade or a rope or a fist. Directly from me. I don't want any confusion.

I am wielding the blade.

I am the one that will control its arc and the depth of its penetration.

I am the one that will withdraw and reinsert the blade, sometimes into a prior wound and sometimes making a fresh incision. Sometimes inserted at an angle just beneath the surface of the skin so that its transparency will reveal the shape of the entire length of the blade, and sometimes plunged into the hilt, until my hand touches his skin and I withdraw the blade in sudden revulsion at the touch.

As I stand there, before I take that step towards him, will he realize, will he know in that moment, if he became silent then, if he looked clearly for a moment directly at me, that he would save his life, that I wouldn't touch him, that I would walk away satisfied, that the moment of hesitation, that moment of silence, would be the sign, the acknowledgement that I seek?

…❧…

BOOK II

PART III

THE YOUNGEST SON

Chapter 1

ENO

CHILDREN sit outside the cinema, backs leaning against the low wall that led to the ticket office. They started lining up at 11:00 am even though the ticket office didn't open until 1:30 p.m. and the film didn't start until 2:00 p.m.

The idea behind arriving so early was to be first in line, so that on purchasing their tickets they could rush through the darkened theater, following the lines of red lights embedded in the floor, to the hallowed spot, the seat that was dead center of the screen, in the very first row, where, with their backs horizontal to the seat cushion, necks jammed between seat and backrest, they could peer up at the screen with the stain of dripping ice-cream and watch Pat Boone, the great, great, great, great grandson of Daniel Boone, win the horse race in 'April Love.'

Outside, while waiting, sat young boys in shorts. In front of most of them were piles of comic books. Batman, Superman, the Hulk, the Hornet, the Fantastic Five, The Silver Surfer, Captain America, Wonder Woman, Scrooge, Goofy, Mickey Mouse, Donald Duck, Hawkman, the Flash, Green Lantern, and Collections of the Classics that included illustrated tales of the Alamo, Captain Silver, and Robin Hood.

Crouched on their haunches or lying splayed out on the hot tar in front of these piles were other young boys, their scrotums puckered and in plain view up the legs of their shorts, large wads of Chappies or Wicks bubblegum stuffed in their mouths as they chanted the sorting litany, "Seen, seen, haven't seen, seen, seen, haven't seen."

Occasionally, two boys sorted through each other's collections at the same time. With the surrounding chorus of other boys all chanting in various incantations of "Seen, seen, haven't seen, seen, seen, haven't seen", the sidewalk in front of the Movie theater bore a cacophonous resemblance to a Middle Eastern Spice or Asian Fish Market. From this apparent disorder filtered the fair exchange of a Superman for a Spiderman, a Captain America for a Hulk, 2 Silver Surfer for one Giant Issue Batman.

With the auditorium in tumult, the simple slides that advertised local businesses faded, and the lights dimmed to the loud cheer of the children. On the screen appeared the logo of the British Movietone News underlined by the cursive text, 'It speaks for itself', and accompanied by strident music eerily similar to Hollywood fanfares heralding Caesar's arrival at the Coliseum of Rome.

Flickering, grainy images in black and white, headlines followed by footage of events scrolled and dissolved on and off the screen accompanied by an off-screen narrator with a distincly Queen's English accent.

Rome Treaty, Common Market Established.

"The Rome Treaty was signed by France, West Germany, Italy, Belgium, the Netherlands and Luxembourg. The treaty establishes the European Economic Community, otherwise known as the Common Market ..."

Mao Said: " Let A Thousand Flowers Bloom ..."

"The Chairman of China's Communist Party, Mao Tse-Tung, delivered a speech in which he stated: 'Let a thousand flowers bloom, a hundred schools of thought contend.' To many observers, these statements seem to show a relaxing of totalitarian rule…"

Federal Troops Integrate Schools in Little Rock, U.S.A.

"After local authorities refused to implement court-ordered desegregation, President Eisenhower ordered federal troops to do the job. He stated: 'I will uphold The Federal Constitution, by every means at my command…'."

Sputnik Launched by Russians

"The Soviet Union launched the first satellite into space. The satellite has a diameter of 22 inches ..."

USSR and US Launch ICBMs

"Both the United States and the USSR successfully launched Intercontinental Ballistic Missiles…"

The narrator delivered the description of these events with melodramatic good cheer or with assumed stately and objective dispassion, including any audience, from Dakar to Oman, from Timbuktu to Tahiti, as if they were the beneficiaries of all productive and uplifting events, the compassionate witnesses of tragedies, the dispassionate observation of the targets of aggression, conveyed through the good graces of Her Majesty, the Queen of England, Elizabeth II, and the benevolence of the British Empire.

The propaganda was lost on the small boys, who, even though the images on screen reflected sharply in their eyes and lit up their faces and open mouths with delicate shadows of contrast.

They waited in the barely held tension of anticipation for that moment that surmounted the fear of the Coyote catching the Roadrunner.

That moment that pierced the glow of pride and strength in Mighty Mouse rescuing Mitzi.

That moment that transcended that squeal of joy at Speedy Gonzales throwing his sombrero in the air and shouting, "Arriba, arriba, arriba, ándale, ándale".

That moment of elation and wonder when Superman said "Up, up and away", at the end of each episode on the radio every weekday at 5:00 pm before Long John Silver and the Radio Record Club.

They waited in the barely held tension of anticipation for that moment that surmounted the fear of the Coyote catching the Roadrunner.

That moment that pierced the glow of pride and strength in Mighty Mouse rescuing Mitzi, that moment that transcended that squeal of joy at Speedy Gonzales throwing his sombrero in the air and shouting, "Arriba, arriba, arriba, ándale, ándale".

That moment of elation and wonder when Superman said, "Up, up and away" at the end of each episode on the radio every weekday at 5:00 pm before Long John Silver and the Radio Record Club.

That moment of anticipation when the cartoon commercial for Eno's Fruit Salts began;

"When you're feeling low, Eno. When you're feeling low, Eno."

That moment..., that moment…, when the end of the commercial depicted 3 windows in a row, when an animated character appeared in each, and successively pulled down the shade in front of each.

That moment when the accompanying song continued, "It's mild and gentle, and good, good tasting."

That moment when, in perfect synchronization, each of the shades of the windows pulled down to reveal each letter, E-N-O.

And the children burst at the seams, let go of all their inhibitions, all their expectations, all their pent-up desires, and screamed, at the top of their lungs, as loud as they could muster their young voices, in perfect rhythm with the song, in perfect synchronicity with the window shades pulling down.

E-N-O!

What a moment.

E–N-O!

…❧…

Shaye rarely participated in the chorus of 'Eno' once he reached age 5. He was assigned to spend every Saturday morning and every school vacation at the family store at the insistence of the Master.

As yet unable to attend customers at that young age, he dipped his hands into the bins of nails, washers and bolts, withdrawing them, black to his elbows, to show he had labored that day and hadn't spent most of the Saturday morning sitting in the corner of the store beside the chicken wire partition at the entrance, staring at the Aston Martin and Studebaker Skylark Dinky toys that were displayed on the shelf.

He dearly wanted those toys, but like much else, he didn't know he could ask for something he desired or needed.

He did know he didn't want to go to the store all those Saturday mornings when the Master entered the darkness of the bedroom, pulled open the curtains, ripped off the covers to floor, saying gruffly, "Get up! It's time to go. Get up!" and left the room with Shaye lying bare and vulnerable on the wrinkled white sheets with the faint outlines of many nights of wetting the bed and vague residues of the previous night getting stoned with his friends by the lake down the road.

When Shaye completed his military service, the Master informed him, without discussion, he and his mother were leaving on yet another three-month international trip and handed him the keys to the store once again.

Shaye, not realizing that this was a test of his competence, dutifully took care of the store in his father's absence, opening the store with its big iron gates, depositing the cash in the bank, ordering the goods, stocking the shelves, and paying the wages.

When the Master returned, without compliment or thanks, he informed the son that he was turning over the store to him, to which Shaye replied, "I want to go to India."

The Master never forgave him for this transgression and often reminded Shaye of it, saying, "I had to sell it to a damn ghatis!"

This isolation, this absence of dialogue, this belief of the Master in the correctness of his trajectory matched equally with the presumption of Shay's compliance with it.

Shaye sat in the corner of a living room, alone, on those Sunday visits he would later discover were to various relatives of the Master and the Madam. There he stared at the plate of candy that sat on the coffee table between himself and the two groups of adults, ladies at the table, the men arrayed on the sofas, until tea was served and when sometimes a woman at the table would notice him and he was offered a slice of cake, or asked if he wanted a candy.

Alone, he endured the pain of his ear attacks without medication or attendance of a doctor, he endured the abuse of Nathan, he endured the emptiness of the blue Anglia station wagon during the multiple visits the Master made to various stores where he purchased stolen goods and grabbed at the store owner's daughters' bodies.

…❧…

Chapter 2

"Daddy burned your pants,"

SHAYE, now age fifteen, lost and suffering from the accumulation of years of catering to other people's definitions of who he was, vainly attempted to locate and establish his personality with little success.

One attempt he made was to copy fads or fashions he had seen in magazines, like those he saw in the Time Magazine photograph of the girl with the long blonde hair and beads dancing in the park in America.

Over time, his clothing came to comprise denim jeans, sandals and shirts with imprinted flowers discarded by Nathan.

Most recently, he had taken to writing on his denim jeans. He wrote words like 'Peace', and 'Love'. He also drew several Ban the Bomb symbols. But mostly he wrote the names of various drugs, LSD, Dexies (Dexedrine), Bennies (Benzedrine), Black Bombs, Purple Hearts.

These names and others similar were scrawled across the now somewhat tattered jeans which he wore at every opportunity, especially on Friday nights when the local youths gathered at the local shopping center to play pinball and glean information about where the parties were being held that weekend

It was on one of those Friday nights that the Masters' supposed closest friend had seen Shaye at the shopping center wearing the denim pants.

On the Saturday afternoon following, Shaye had returned home from an outing to find Rebecca both agitated and pale.

"Daddy burned your pants," she reported.

To Shaye, the burning of the pants, his naïve attempt at transmitting his own sense of how other people should see him, was crushed by the weight of his father's own need for the same.

As had been the case since he was a small child, in a ritual of generations, fathers will sublimate their sons in a perpetual re-enactment of the rituals of circumcision, the subjugation to Master, to Father, to God, over and over.

This was the same void of the Other the Master tried to fill by substituting the cheap whiskey in the bottle of Glenlivet, or by accepting the compliments for the chips that Ettie actually made, or by parading his angst in revenge on Shaye for inscribing the Madam's maiden name on her tombstone, until he, aged, half blind and almost deaf, became that same void filled with such quantity of vacuous substitutions that it sagged at the weight of indifference suspended between two points.

...❧...

Chapter 3

The Erasure of Trust

THE Beretta pistol would be handy on that day of 'The Revolution' but otherwise never left its place except on those days that Shaye pulled out each of the drawers of the cupboard to form a staircase to the uppermost cupboard where the Beretta lay.

Here is where he sat silently in the darkness of the confined space, feeling the weight of the gun in his small hand, turning it over, turning the safety switch off and on, off and on, turning it over, side to side.

...❧...

SHAYE was quite familiar with the staircase of drawers.

In the house with the circle window with the shadow of the palm tree, Shaye formed the staircase to get to the uppermost cupboard from which he launched

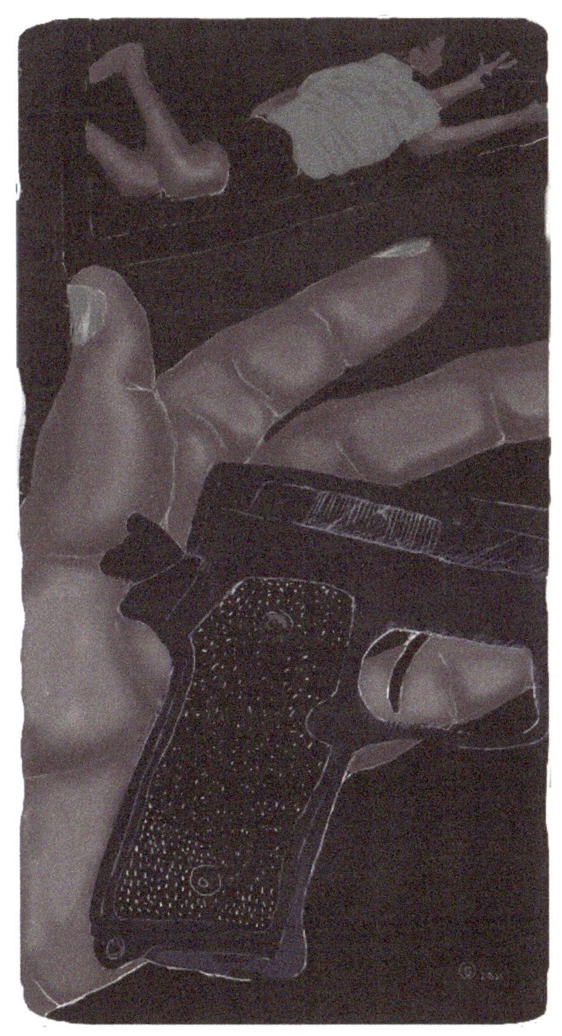

... turning it over, turning the safety switch off and on ...

himself into unconsciousness by diving headfirst into the down cover he had placed as a cushion at the foot of the staircase.

He was quite familiar with that unconsciousness as well.

As a young child Shaye's first experience with unconsciousness began with him holding a bottle of Mercurochrome disinfectant. Nathan wanted the bottle for himself. But Shaye refused to give it over, which caused Nathan to chase him, which made Shaye run away.

Nathan, already a victim of familial obesity at that age, realizing that Shaye was faster than he, shouted, "Close your eyes!", which Shaye did, and promptly ran straight into a wall, knocking himself unconscious.

The now broken Mercurochrome bottle slashed a deep cut on his forehead, and thus produced the first part of 'The Cross'.

This was not only the young boys' first experience of unconsciousness, but also of the consequences of conflicts between what is said and what is meant. The erasure of trust, the sense of betrayal, began that day.

His next experience of unconsciousness also formed the second part of 'The Cross', adding yet another layer of association to the erasure of trust, the sense of betrayal, to be scratched at.

This time it was Rebecca's friend who wanted to play 'Helicopter'. She told Shaye to lie face down on the sidewalk, took him by the ankles and swung him around and around, around and around, around and around, around and around, until wobbling with giddiness, arms burning and weak with strain, she finally let go of his ankles, mid-swing, whereupon the small boy finally experienced, once more, that moment of freedom, that flight that he later only experienced in sleep and dreams, and where he finally, once again, experienced unconsciousness by flying directly into the corner edge of a low brick wall.

Mercurochrome

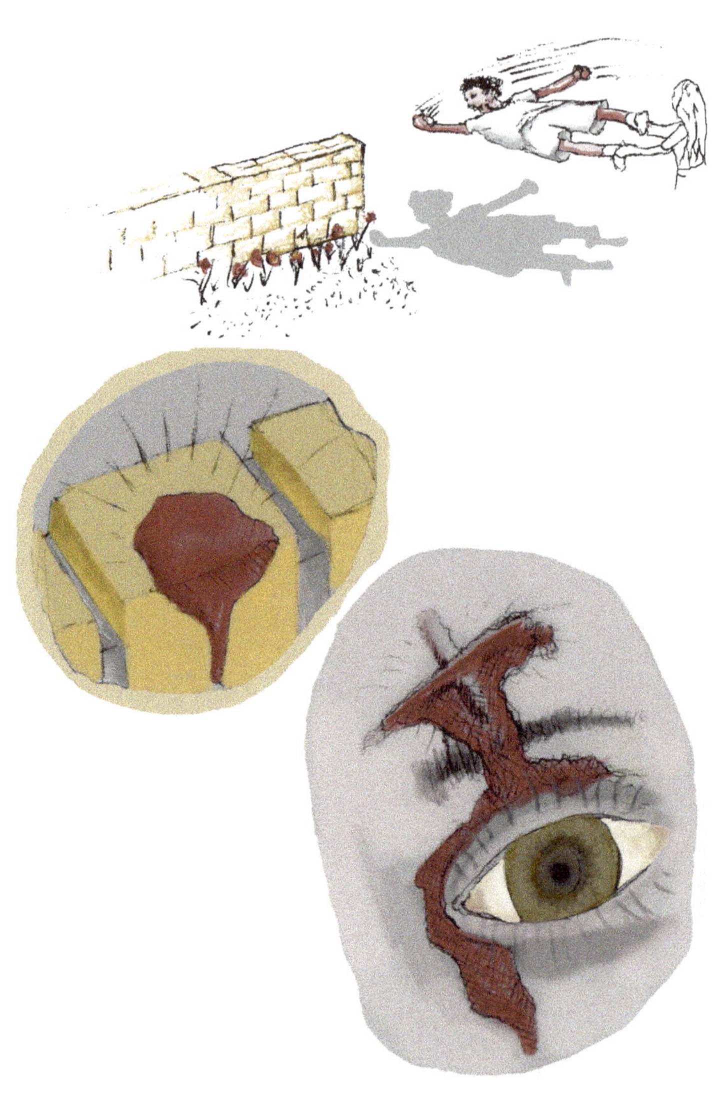

... around and around, around and around ...

... the staircase to get to the uppermost cupboard ...

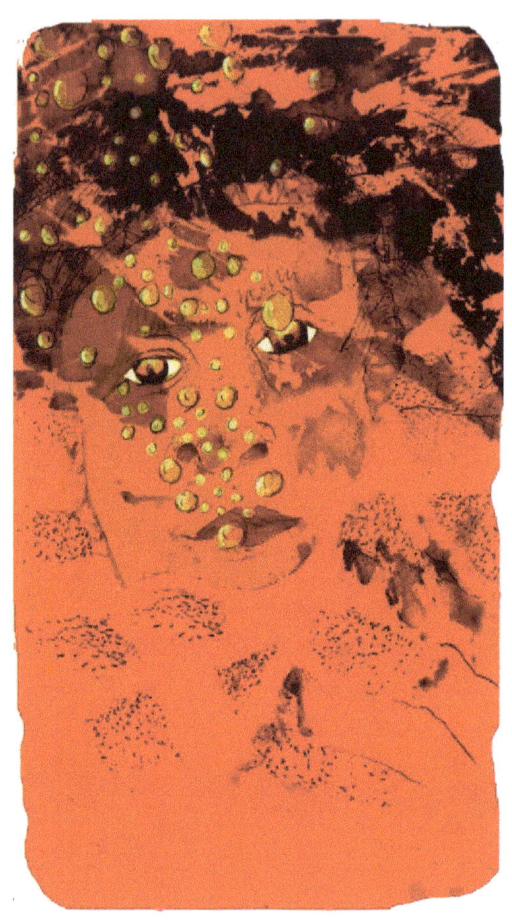

... the young boy struggled underwater ...

The horizontal gash that formed into a heavy scar on healing, together with the heavy vertical scar that formed from the gash caused by the breaking Mercurochrome bottle, formed 'The Cross,' that sign of 'the Other,' the sign that had such significance, part of the load the Madam and generations before her carried again and again.

Within a year, the Madam arranged for Shaye to undergo plastic surgery and have 'The Sign' removed. She didn't want her Jewish son to bear a Cross his entire life.

Once again, in surgery, he experienced that transition to unconsciousness, that spiral as the Pentothal took hold, that void that appeared, so similar to the one that appeared that afternoon when the uncle threw him in the swimming pool wrapped in a blanket and laughed as the young boy struggled underwater to wrestle his way out of the heavy wet blanket.

So similar to the imaginings he had of the experience of ending his life by suicide, or what it felt like at the moment of death, your body crashing against the concrete as you fell from a great height.

So similar to the envelope of mist and darkness, as your organs failed and the vibration of the last gasp of your brain, starved of blood, reached a sudden climax before succumbing to the overdose.

Added to that day is another layer of association to the erasure of trust, the sense of betrayal to be scratched over time. Somehow, all these factors coalesced in his experience. These were his markers, these experiences became his points of orientation.

. . . ❧ . . .

He held a towel above his head as he ran as fast as he could off the end of his grandmother's garage roof and plunged into unconsciousness rather than floating down gently in breathless and silent joy. He held his breath until he trembled from the force of the exertion as the pain of the pressure building behind his ear drums progressed through the night to the point of intolerance where the only relief lay in bashing his head against the wall, or in cupping his hand and slapping it against his ear in the vain hope of bursting the infected eardrum, or in hoping that the Madam would at least administer some

... he ran as fast as he could ...

Aspirin to relieve some of the pain, or that the Madam would overcome her notions of social courtesy and call the Doctor, even though it was the middle of the night.

He held his breath until he trembled from the force of the exertion while the doctor pumped hot water up the transparent tubes inserted unknown to him in the operation the week before, that now seated in the Doctor's office, extended from the young boys nose like tusks of a great African elephant and then drained into the silver kidney bowl he held below his chin, the yellow globs of infected mucous floating inches from his eyes.

He blew his breath into the mouth of his lover, and she returned it into his, until they both exhausted the oxygen and they trembled from the force of their effort, and then as if from behind a drawn curtain they floated in silence in the void that appeared and permeated them as their genitals pulsed in and around each other.

He lay on the floor, on his side, his knees drawn into his chest as he beat himself on the head with his hands and then his fists until it became clear what a senseless gesture towards his pain this was, at which point the silence descended and the void opened, until, breathless, with no force, no dramatic excision, that voice appeared, lonely and distant, approaching every moment with more confidence in its own presence, until finally it overwhelmed the body, until it finally expressed itself fully as the wailing banshee it was, pained and lonely in its nostalgia for the emptiness of the void, anguished in its confused solitude and anxiety at knowing the world.

In this, the Madam and her youngest son shared the same worlds.

...❧...

SHAYE hadn't always been lonely. He had friends before.

The hole in the wire fence to the house of the two young girls next door, the rivulets in the mud after the storm.

The balance of the broomstick at the point of his finger.

The greasy black underside of the yellow Ford Zephyr.

The switch that turned on the fountain in the swimming pool, the valve that emptied the air from the water filter tank with a hiss.

The heat of the scalding pale green water in the bathtub that rose from the surface and misted the bathroom so all mirrors were hidden.

In the bath, the water steadily grew cold and then drained ever so slowly from the plug he had displaced slightly until he was left naked and exposed in the empty tub, staring at his stretched reflection in the chrome spout. Friends, intimate friends.

There was also the day that occasional small trickles of blood joined the last residues of the receding pale green water as he bled from the multiple minuscule cuts inflicted by the hand razor he used to shave the faint soft white down of hair from his entire body.

Many afternoons he climbed to the roof of the house, walked up the clay terracotta roof tiles, sat on its peaked roof and reached with his stare towards the water tower on the far-off hill not knowing that his mother, the Madam, would be buried near to that tower one day, and where he stood next to her tombstone and reached back towards that orange terracotta roof above the koppies and the lake in the distance.

He never shared this perch with anyone else. He invited no one to join him there, nor did he let anyone know where he was or of the danger of climbing to such heights.

No-one asked what he had learned in school that day, and where he had learned nothing besides that the Ice Cream 'Boy' with the three wheeled bicycle cart hadn't wanted his plain jam sandwiches in trade for an Eskimo Pie.

No-one asked where he had been after school that day, or any other day.

Not the days when he played soccer with a tennis ball for hours with the Christian and the Portuguese boy until darkness forced him to remember it was a quarter to six and his father would be home any minute.

Not the days when he sat on the sidelines of the soccer or cricket field of the school and watched the children in their school colors score goals or runs, and jump on their bicycles afterward, their studded boots hanging by their laces around their necks, ringing their bells or yelling at each other as they braked hard and skidded in the playground's dirt, throwing up clouds of orange dust they carried home in their hair and socks.

No-one asked who had given him the small pillow of 'Snap', one of the Kellogg's Rice Krispies trio, Snap Crackle and Pop, nor what he had asked the Magic Robot that always answered his question correctly.

No-one asked which tree he had climbed to get to the figs, or the plums, nor which drain had scraped his shin as he crawled in to recover the worn tennis ball.

No-one asked why he had crawled under the house to sit with the metal horse with the pedals lying on its side in the stale dust, nor what had happened to his pants with the dried white residue of a wide urine stain at the crotch.

Nor was there any question about his relationships in the future with its certain perversity in the incestuous nature of his participation.

He tolerated his abuse in silence until he could transform the silence into a certain distance, silent but far less damaging to himself, a distance where, at the periphery of his vision, he could watch the blurred movement of their lips and hear nothing at all besides the occasional mutter of indistinguishable sounds that might or might not have been words.

In that manner, he he tried to free himself from the burden of carrying their abuse, which he had incorporated into himself, to where their abuse of him was the same abuse with which he abused himself.

He unwrapped the garbage bags and threw their wrapping inside one of the garbage bags.

He cleaned the vacuum cleaner with the vacuum cleaner.

The mirror appeared as the condensation withdrew.

The prisoners were forced to break a pile of stones into smaller pieces, carry the broken stones from one side of Robben Island to the other, bury them, dig them up again, and carry them back to the unbroken pile.

Jews dug their own graves for the Nazis.

Two atoms collide.

...❧...

Chapter 4

The Storm

SHAYE experienced a similar but more crucial dilemma than the one caused by the box of cereal, one that often leveraged his self-worth to either side of the pendulum of circumstance. He was barely 19 years old, having returned from his mandatory army conscription when he applied for a 'Manager Trainee' position at the African Division of an English Water Reservoir company.

To his surprise, he was hired. After a short period of drawing plans at the headquarters, a site foreman suggested to the office manager they might make better use of Shaye out in the field.

On arrival at the construction site, a large area on the top of a small koppie, the Englishman foreman sent the boy out of the office trailer to the adjoining work site, saying to him as he closed the door on the blast of heat that blew in, "Make sure they keep working".

Nothing more than that, simply, "Make sure they keep working."

Shaye approached the work site to find a mound of dirt eight feet high surrounding a hundred-foot diameter trench dug about three feet wide and some four feet into the red dirt. Standing in line, in the trench, each about four feet from the other, worked a crew of some forty men with pickaxes.

The men were barely dressed, most of them bare-chested, without shoes or chest hair, most with only a tattered pair of ragged shorts, their bodies shining almost to the point of transparency, with sweat as their only reflector of the intense rays of the sun.

As Shaye stood on top of the mound of dirt, the sound of the men's singing voices drifted towards him. Somewhere amongst the 40 men, a single voice was calling the words to a song. That sentence, or parts of a sentence, Shaye never knew which as he couldn't understand their language, repeated in unison by all the men, at the end of which they again shouted in unison, one word or one exclamation as they brought down their pick axes like a large convulsing centipede crawling in the rivulets formed in the red dirt, 'Shaya!'.

The men stood upright again, some of them spitting into the palms of their hands or rubbing on the necks of the pick axes as the solitary voice of the leader sang the next part, and the men waited, leaning slightly on the necks of the pickaxes, their heads staring down at the dirt in front of them as they joined in the repetitious phrase sung in a lilting but powerful voice. Some made a slight shuffle of their feet or a gentle pounding of the heel of one foot in anticipation, and then again, in unison they lifted the pick axes and brought them solidly over their shoulders in one gentle arching curve and stuck and then pierced the red dirt in front of them accompanied by their loud exclamation, 'Shaya!'

And then, a section of the men's voices broke away into another rhythm of synchronous words or low throated exhaust, or sometimes simply the loud vibration of tongues, or a high pitched short yell, or a whistle, or the clapping of hands together, or hand slapped against wet thighs, until that rhythm would counterpoint the isolation of the voice of the leader and then follow the unison of the other voices until together they would oscillate in a polyphonic contrapuntal dance that would sometimes syncopate in rhythm and sometimes not, until this all climaxed and repeated with the word, once again, 'Shaya!', and the pickaxes fell.

As the afternoon progressed, so did the intensity of the heat, burning away any traces of the storm that had come in so suddenly from the east with its enormous clumsy puffy black clouds edged with brilliant white.

The storm had been drawing in for some time, appearing first as a slightly dark discoloration of the thin blue sky at the edges of the far away koppies, then racing across the bright yellow veld in a dark shadow highlighted with intense flashes of forked lightning and rolling thunder as the veil between storm and heat drew overhead, pummeling the tall grass to the ground with large globules of rain until all the fine seed heads bowed in submission and the storm passed just as suddenly as it had appeared leaving behind the rolling valleys and the bare thorn trees steaming with gentle wisps of vapor rising to dissipate in the weight of the now wet air..

The men had continued working and singing with only the occasional glance towards the impending storm until the storm was right upon them, water cascading onto their shoulders from their heads, and then, suddenly, they all broke ranks and scattered in a chaotic mass to anything they could find shelter under.

Some sat on their haunches under the eaves of the trailer, while others gathered under a small tarpaulin cover pulled from a concrete mixer. Another group gathered under another canvas tarpaulin pulled from a large compressor. Those that couldn't find shelter simply sat on their haunches in the rain, heads down, their arms gathered over their heads, waiting out the storm on the mound of red dirt now drawn with dark veins.

The aperture of the sun struggled to pierce the substance of the fast-moving clouds and finally broke out behind the storm as the edge of the wave of grey shadow receded across the landscape replaced once again by the bright yellow grass popping back upright in staccato pinpoints of strobing light patterns rolling across the veldt.

The men, once again, formed a cohesive group, left their meager shelters and walked slowly and in silence towards the trench.

They gathered once more in the trench, in line, in order, gathered up their pick axes and waited, many glancing about, some wiping their brow with their fingers and with a snap of the wrist shedding the water, some simply staring ahead at the ground once again, leaning on the shaft of the pickaxe, until, again, that solitary voice rose above the few mutterings and the slight squish of toes in what had become red mud, and the voice of the leader sang the next part, and the men waited as they joined in the repetition, some with a slight bending at the waist or a gentle side to side tilt of their heads, and then, again, in unison, as they sang the chorus, they lifted the pick axes until the points of the axes almost touched the skin of their backs, and, in one gentle arching curve, brought them solidly over their shoulders and stuck and then pierced deep into the red mud in front of them.

'Shaya!'

Shaye, on seeing the oncoming storm, had left his perch on the mound and positioned himself comfortably under the entrance to the trailer, from where he witnessed the rise and fall of the storm and the scattering and reformation of the workers in the trench.

Once again, crouched on the red mound of dirt surrounding the trench, he watched as instructed as the men worked the trench with their pickaxes.

'Shaya!'

'Shaya!'

'Shaya!'

Now and then, as Shaye shifted his weight on his haunches, a stream of dirt, sometimes accompanied by a few larger clods, flowed down the side of the mound and bounced and scattered in the trench below. Sometimes the dirt also poured slightly onto the workers below and occasionally a larger clod rolled and came to rest at, or touching, their heel or toe.

A man, some ten years older than him, positioned in the trench some feet below, almost directly below Shaye.

After about half an hour of labor following the interruption of the storm, the man paused, and resting his axe against his hip, he unwrapped the soiled cloth that he had bound carefully to the axe handle and mopped his face and his shaved bald head.

Shaye, atop the mound, watched immobile as the man wiped his shoulders and then his arms.

The man looked up, and as if noticing each other for the first time, their eyes met across continents of journeys and expeditions, in a confluence of generations and genders, in a mesh of cultures and characters.

Without pause, without the slightest jolt or shiver, without a change in expression or posture, without gulping or shifting, the young boy sitting on his haunches, his tall boots biting at his calves and his arm rested on his knee, simply swiveled his hand at the wrist and casually pointed with his finger at the man's pickaxe, motioning for the man to return to work.

…❧…

THAT moment, that gesture, that casual flick of the wrist.

That moment as he hit the wall, bottle in hand.

That moment, when he knew there was no going back as he propelled himself forward from a great height.

That moment when the present most obviously was the cusp where the past flowed into the future.

That moment, struck by the oncoming vehicle, just before the shroud of unconsciousness overwhelmed him.

That moment when the wet blanket clung just too tight, and he gave up struggling as he drew the first breath of water through the gauze of the blanket.

At that moment, 'E–N-O'.

That moment when she couldn't tolerate the cold water or the inconclusivity of her thoughts any longer, and pulled herself out of the bathtub and left her husband.

That moment when a minuscule slice of passing history became concretized, crystallized, transfixed.

That moment when the child says, "Daddy, you don't play with us like you used to."

Where is the point that habit fails, where ritual falls out of alignment and it comes to consciousness that things just aren't what they once were, that things have changed and most often for the worse?

Where is the point of that fulcrum, what is the factor that adds the weight to that one side, that makes the balance shift, where the weight transfers, where when what's implied becomes inferred, becomes whole, assumes full form, abstract or concrete, verbalized or subliminal, where the load slides across the platform of experience and crashes into the side of conflict?

That moment when, only by asking, the answer reveals itself.

. . . ~ . . .

THE man simply remained motionless for that moment, as did Shaye. Their eyes fixed on each other while transmitting their wavelengths of history and culture, of power and submission, back and forth, back and forth.

A smile grew at the edges of the man's mouth and then crossed his face in a broad expression.

Without breaking their momentary fixed stare, in a completely intuitive motion, without looking, at his waist, the man gathered, then twisted the cloth about the handle of the axe, lifted the pick axe above his head until the point of the pickaxe again almost touched the skin of his back, then he paused, and, in one gentle arching curve, still smiling broadly, brought the pick axe solidly over his shoulder and stuck and then pierced deep into the red mud in front of him.

'Shaya!'

Indelibly etched in the mirror of the young boy's experience are the politics of that moment, that flick of the wrist.

'Shaya!'

That image on the back of the box of cereal mirrored his mother's reflection of herself.

'Shaya!'.

Some would have said that she lived a life of luxury in her house full of rooms and servants and dreams, but in fact, it was a living hell for her.

'Shaya!'.

…❧…

BOOK III

BEI MIR BIST DU SCHON

(YOU ARE BEAUTIFUL TO ME)

Music by Sholom Secunda, cousin of the Master.
Original lyrics by Jacob Jacobs.
with Saul Chaplin and Sammy Cahn

Ven di zolst zayn shvarts vi a tuter,
ven di host oygn vi bay a kuter
un ven di hinkst tsibislekh,
host hiltserne fislekh,
zug ikh, dus art mikh nit.
Un ven di host a narishn shmeykhl
un ven di host Vayzusyes seykhl,
ven di bist vild vi indianer,
bist afile a galitsyaner,
zug ikh, dus art mikh nit.
Zug mikh, vi erklersti dus?
Khvel dir zugn bald farvus:
Bay mir bisti sheyn.
Bay mir hosti kheyn.
Bist eyne bay mir oyf der velt.
Bay mir bisti git.
Bay mir hosti "it."

Bay mir bisti tayerer fin gelt
Fil sheyne meydlekh hobn shoyn
gevolt nemen mikh
un fin zey ale oysgeklibn
hob ikh nor dikh.
Bay mir bisti sheyn.
Bay mir hosti kheyn.
Bist eyne bay mir oyf der velt.
Bei mir bist du schön - please let me explain,
Bei mir bist du schön means that you're grand.
Bei mir bist du schön, again I'll explain.
It means you're the fairest in the land.
I could say, "Bella, bella,"
Even say "voonderbar."
Each language only helps me tell you
How grand you are.
I've tried to explain "bei mir bist du schön,"
So kiss me and say you understand.

... ...

BOROUGH MOTHER PRAYS FOR SON WHO SOLD SONG HIT FOR $30

- Brooklyn Eagle, December 24, 1937

Each morning Mrs. Anna Secunda, 76, leaves her small home at 268 1/2 Penn St. for a synagogue on the corner, where she spends the day in fasting and prayer to atone for the mistake of her son, Sholem, who sold the song hit of the day for $30.

Mrs. Secunda, who speaks no English, does not understand contracts and the law. She only knows that her son five years ago wrote a song called "Bei Mir Bist Du Schoen", which today is making a fortune for its publishers, J. and J. Kammen. Secunda yielded his rights in 1933. Sammy Kahn and Saul Chaplin put English lyrics to it and revised it into swing tempo early this Summer and the rest is making tin pan alley history.

Freely translated, 'Bei Mir Bist Du Schoen' means 'You Are Beautiful to Me.'

But his mother believes that somewhere along the years of her life, which began in Russia, she has sinned against God, and her son is being punished. Sholem, who lives at 86 Avenue A, Manhattan, this morning tried to explain laws of copyright to his mother because she planned to go back to the synagogue today and he fears her frail body may not withstand the fast.

Ms. C. BARRY: "The song's original composer, Sholom Secunda, was already legendary for an earlier career blunder: telling a young George Gershwin to take a hike when the two set up as a songwriting team. Gershwin changed the course of Western popular music. Secunda sold "Bei Mir Bist Du Schoen" for $30. This may be the only surviving recording of Sholom Secunda's voice, a 1962 interview on radio station WEVD in New York."

Mr. SHOLOM SECUNDA (Composer): "I thought that $30 was a pretty good sum of money for a song that's not doing well."

Unidentified Woman #5: "I agree."

Mr. SECUNDA: "So, I thought, give me the $30, and here's the song. My mother was the one who suffered the most. She, being a very pious woman, felt that she must have sinned and that I am paying for her sins. And she went very often to the synagogue just to pray. One day, she made up her mind she's going to stay in the synagogue all day and pray and fast and maybe God will help her and I will be recognized for the song."

Unidentified Woman #5: "Well, now I'm afraid our time has run out. But before it really goes all the way, I think this would be a very good time to listen to the song we love so well in its newest arrangement, which is by Steve Lawrence and Eydie Gorme, "Bei Mir Bist Du Schoen."

... ❧ ...

Chapter 1

Du Bist Schon

THE Master, whose relative had written that song, whom he tried to contact on his visit to New York in 1956, kept a small key chain in his bedside drawer, together with the remnants of chocolate and the identity book of the Syrian soldier, his cousin, the Speaker of the House, had given him.

The key chain had what at first looked like a coin between two support posts. Actually, it was a silver disc with a mysterious set of hieroglyphics engraved on each side.

If one flicked the disc, it spun until the markings on both sides merged, and the uninterpretable hieroglyphics, with the magic of persistence of vision, formed the sentence "KUSH MIR IN TOCHES" a Yiddish expression loosely translated as 'Kiss My Ass'.

This was not an unusual expression for a culture that had similar phrases in its lexicon: "Nobody ever lost money making a profit."

Or in attitude towards business transactions: "You don't eat a salami all at once. You eat, but slice by slice."

Where the businessman says: "In my experience, in my business, even the biggest crooks still wanted to be treated fairly."

Where a mother, a holocaust survivor, tells the principal calling her about the bad behavior of her child: "Call me only when you have good news, bad news I don't want!"

Where her husband, also a holocaust survivor, has to leave the house of his daughter and her children, saying, "I can't listen to the crying of the children!"

Where the grandson says, "The history, not one month, not one year, not ten years, one hour! It makes me so sad!"

. . . ❧ . . .

Chapter 2

Sex, Drugs and Conspiracies

THE Madam vaguely remembered when she took up on her friend's advice and asked another friend, the wife of a pharmacist, to ask her husband to supply her with the pills. This request did not surprise him, as he had many other requests from the various ladies in the neighborhood.

From then on, once a month, usually on a Friday, he delivered a package to her about the size of a shoebox. He filled her regular prescriptions plus any new ones she had called in to him. Pills to sleep, pills to stay awake. Appetite suppressant pills, anti-water retention pills, arthritis pills, rheumatism pills, diabetes pills, pain killing pills, and so on.

The pharmacist was a tall and large man, married to a woman that her husband, the Master, was quite attracted to.

A few years later, for some reason no one else was aware of, she no longer had him fill her prescriptions and changed to another pharmacist friend. This pharmacist was tiny and very thin and her husband was attracted to this pharmacist's wife as well. Both pharmacists were also balding at an early age, were rather paunchy, and both delivered their packages to her on their way home from work, usually on Fridays, once a month.

Occasionally, the delivery of medications by the pharmacists coincided with the delivery of farm-fresh eggs to the families' paint, hardware and household goods store by a customer. When that occurred, the pharmacist would deliver the package of prescriptions and leave with two dozen eggs for his wife and children.

Eggs had a special place in the Master's sometimes sharp recollections and sometime fantasies of his past. Eggs reminded him of his mother's sister.

...❧...

HIS mother's sister and her husband had been egg and hide merchants back in the old country where they had become wealthy, trading with France mainly, where some of their family would emigrate to later.

However, everything went awry when the Russian Communists came to power and sent them off, penniless, to Siberia for re-education.

As the train pulled out of the station of the small village, the husband called out from the train window to his little nephew standing on the railway platform;

"The money is under the tree!" he shouted above the cacophony of hissing steam, muffled sobbing and the clattering squealing iron wheels on the bumpy rails.

No one found out under which tree the money was buried, or if anyone had tried to find the tree and the money buried there, or even if this frantic and desperate message had actually occurred.

Perhaps this was just another mythology passed down through the generations. So many families have tales of buried treasure.

As fate would have it, losing their wealth and their internment in Siberia saved their lives. A scant few years later, almost the entire village population was executed in the nearby forest or taken away to concentration camps and later executed there.

Except for the little nephew who heard the message, "The money is under the tree!".

The little nephew, now in his late teens, had escaped the concentration camp and joined the resistance in the forests that surrounded the camp. Later, he went back into the camp and helped his mother, brother and sister escape under the fence. He was a hero.

…❧…

SHE was alone with the death of the child. No one acknowledged the child any longer. Either through embarrassment or courtesy, or their own similar circumstance, no-one mentioned the child's name in her presence.

For her the residues remained, the mark on the cloth where the coffee spilled, the missing glass from the set of four, the dark smudge along the passage wall, above four feet.

But he is gone now.

How could she ever withstand knowing that he is gone forever this time, could only reappear in dreams or in passing moments of reflection, times when he emerged from the faded background of her experience and weighted her emotions so she almost bent over at the waist under the load of that exposure?

Sometimes she recognized that the child had died. Sometimes she recognized that the child had lived.

When those moments occurred, she had wanted to run out and look for the child among the living, look for the child amongst the dead, but she returned to herself in tears and frustration that rose to anger. The aim of her search had become immersed in the process of desperate searching, and hopelessness had won out over patience.

Her husband, in a misaligned effort to help her, pointed out she was acting like her mother, to which she responded in the manner of her mother and lashed out at him.

The mirror looked at itself.

Two atoms collide.

The metal horse with the plastic pedals lies on it's side.

…⁂…

THE child died, the egg and hide merchants were saved, as was the little nephew.

The merchants, now 're-educated', returned to the old country after the war, penniless and childless.

Both died there some years later, with bare belongings and a few faded photographs that were eventually lost somehow but might be somewhere on the Rembrandtsplein market in Amsterdam or the Camden Passage market in Islington.

The little nephew immigrated to a new country where he eventually became the Speaker of the House of Parliament, and declared, "I will do anything for my country! Even support Fascists!".

Some of the other villagers were also saved by leaving the village before the Russian Communists, the German Nazis, or the Lithuanian, Latvian and Ukrainian thugs, came pounding on the doors of the village.

The villagers were aided in this decision mainly by the attempts of various international powers to conscript the local village men into their armies for lengthy periods.

First the Polish came, then the White Russians, then the Red Russians.

Then the Polish again, then the Lithuanian Nationalists and on and on, again and again, each attempting to conscript the men of the village into their armies for ten years or more.

At the beginning, the men did their best to resist conscription simply by faking physical medical ailments. Others walked around with large grins and whistled constantly in feigned mental disorders,

Another method was to fake birth dates.

By the time some men eventually left the village, they were well beyond conscription age, conceptual and official 35-year-olds disguised in the physical bodies of teenagers.

This bureaucratic ruse didn't always work. There were many occasions when the men of the village would have to flee urgently to the surrounding forest to avoid the armies, the same forest where many from the village were later slaughtered.

On one occasion, two of the teenagers crept back into the village to find food and were discovered by the occupying forces. They were both put up against the wall to be shot.

Standing there in the cold wind and silence, quietly muttering their last prayers, the silence only punctuated by the short cough of one captor as he held his rifle to his shoulder, one teenager suddenly bolted and ran off down an alley, his captors shouting and cursing at his heels, unable to draw a bead on the escaping boy as he zigzagged around and over the piles of trash and bodies.

This left the other teenager standing, trembling, staring, now wide eyed at the mortar of a chipped brick wall, red brick he remembered later.

On realizing that he was alone and unguarded, he promptly took off in the opposite direction back to his family, waiting anxiously and hungrily in the forest.

The other teenager, who ran away and saved the other's life, despite his attempt to save his own, or perhaps at the expense of his own, simply disappeared. His family waited some hours in the forest for his return but then had to move on to safer locations, the occasional bursts of gunshots in the distance, no sign of anyone's fate.

So the little nephew was saved, and the egg and hide merchants were saved, and the teenager who hadn't tried to escape was saved.

The teenager was saved once more when a man appeared in the village one day offering to transport people to France. This same man, and several others just like him, were visiting several other villages in the area and surrounding towns and even some of the surrounding countries, offering passage to any destination people wanted to go to. The United States, England, Holland, Sweden, anywhere.

The teenager wanted to go to France. His sister and her husband, the egg and hide merchants, had contacts there that could be helpful in starting a new life without the constant fear of capture, conscription, or death.

Pooling the money from several related families, they put enough money together to purchase a single ticket. Several other families in the village also pooled their money together in this way so that eventually a substantial group of young men, some married, some married with children, some single, all designated representatives of various groups, were ready to leave the village for their various destinations.

Together with the most minimal of personal possessions, various small packages of food packed by their wives, mothers, or neighbors, and tiny bits of gold or a few notes of currency secreted in a sock or in the inner rim of a hat, they boarded the train to the harbor.

There were no streamers flying, cheers called, waving hands or tears on the cheeks of family or friends, children or grandparents as the boat departed the dock. They were already many hours away from the village and the goodbyes at the train station had been draining. The slightest glimpse or touch on a cheek or hand could have left the entire group in an emotional puddle amongst the tracks. But somehow they all held on, like they had done so often in the past. The group of young men wouldn't see their families for two or more years and some they would never see again.

There was no joy in this departure. There was no enthusiasm for the opportunities of this new life in France, or England, or Sweden. They bore with them the load of generations that had gone on the same or similar journeys. The edges had become faded and ragged, the threads barely hanging together. Yet they had no other alternative but to bear the load, save enough money to send back to the family so that one more person could purchase a ticket to make this miserable journey. So that together, the two of them could save enough money to send back to the family so that another one, perhaps two or three or four or eventually a whole family, could purchase tickets to make this miserable journey.

After several days on the water, some of the young men began getting suspicious about the journey. No one had seen the men who had sold them the tickets since the day they delivered the tickets to the village with directions to a port.

On asrrival, it seemed peculiar to some of them that no matter what the final destination was, everyone had boarded the same boat. As none of them could speak the language of the crew to make inquiries, they were left to their own devices until the day came when they arrived at what turned out to be the final and only destination of the boat.

Africa.

The men who had sold them the tickets had been double dipping. The British Government of this country in Africa was paying the men to bring anyone they could to the country as long as they were not black.

Eastern European, Western European, Northern European, Southern European, Greek or Portuguese, Latvian or Lithuanian, English, Scottish or Welsh, Northern or Southern Irish, Dutch or French or Belgian. Italians from the Alpine region or Swiss from the same. Laborer or financier, criminal or historian, old or young, disabled or not, without regard to culture or religion, financial standing or class, color of eyes, shape of skull, thickness of hair or length of leg, aptitude for mechanics or medicine, languages or history, nothing mattered except that you were not black.

The government paid the ticket sellers for each immigrant.

The families paid them for each immigrant.

Lithuania became France.

France became Africa.

Eggs or hides.

Journeys from train stations on the plateau or the steppes.

Journeys across oceans without Yiddish names, subject to storms, shipwrecks, sicknesses without description, and deaths compounded over centuries..

Arriving at a port that appeared out of the haze of an early morning mist with the grandeur of the huge flat-topped mountain with clouds spread across its top edge and spilling over its slopes in a waterfall of white vapor that disappeared as it feathered into the rising heat of the sun baked city below unlike anything they had experienced before.

It didn't matter.

They still bore the weight of their history, the clatter of their genes struggling for dominance or submission.

There was no joy at this vista of opportunity.

It was still a miserable journey.

…❧…

WHEN the pharmacist left the package of prescriptions on the dinner table and left the house with the two dozen eggs for his wife and children, this sounded a very particular resonance for the husband of the Madam.

A tray of eggs held the residue of many layers of significance for the Master. He would draw in a large breath at seeing a tray of eggs and breath out ever so slowly. The eggs are more fragile than ever. The weight of the load to bear was always there and he would pass the load onto his sons and daughter and they to theirs.

It was his father who was that 'old' teenager. It was his father who was the teenager, who had run away and saved the other teenager's life, despite his attempt to save his own, or perhaps at the expense of his own.

It was his father who had made that miserable journey to 'France'.

…❧…

Chapter 3

Chips

OCCASIONALLY, the Master has offered me potato chips he had made. Cold, soggy chips, frozen and then thawed, probably several times.

"C'mon, have some. I made them especially for you," he said.

The chips, soaked in liberal quantities of vinegar and smothered in salt, tasted like cardboard dipped in sour water. During my visit, I've tried to avoid touching or ingesting anything he has made or that comes out of the moldy refrigerator.

Today is Friday. The Master's 'seeing eye', as he refers to his aide, was here this morning. Ettie, her non-seeing eye name, came and cooked a large plate full of fresh chips. Fluffy chips made with fresh oil and fresh white potatoes, both of which she had brought with her.

She left at 12:00.

At 12:10, the director of the facility and the social worker came up to the apartment to say goodbye to me and to thank me for the workshop I had done yesterday.

The Master offered them the fresh Ettie chips. All four of us are standing facing each other in a loose circle.

“Hm, these chips are good,” said the social worker.

“Aren’t they!!! Who made them?,” said the director, addressing the Master.

Avoiding the question, the Master replied, “Here have another ..., dip it in this onion and tomato sauce…”, (that Ettie had also made.)

“Oh, you are such an excellent cook,” said the social worker once again addressing the Master.

“Isn’t he just an incredible cook?,” the director says to me, one chip in her mouth and another ready in her hand.

The Master stood silently with the plate of chips, smiling from ear to ear.

They left, and the Master says to me, without smiling and in a completely different tone of voice, "See, they like me."

…❧…

Chapter 4

Sex

THE Master thought he looked like Frank Sinatra. He did, but his ears were too large, as was his nose. And he spoke with a lisp that rolled the letter 'R' as a low vibration.

The Master revealed to his now mature children that on the day he was born, as his mother carried him home down the main street of his small home town, his father had passed in the opposite direction, with the body of his two-year-old elder sister on its way to burial.

"She died of malnutrition," the Master said.

None of this tale made factual sense. It was one of those peculiarly obtuse moments when the Master reached an unintentional eloquence in relating this mythos of life taken and life given again, of the transformative means of faith and the consuming envelope of tragedy.

Occasionally, the Master, in his later years, would relate moments of his life with unexpected urgency and candor. Sometimes he disregarded decorum, and often fact and fiction became interchangeable as well, as in the myth about the death of his sister.

Sometimes the raw truth of his secret life broke out of the mist of the past, out from behind the newspaper at the dinner table, into the forum of old age and bitterness.

…❧…

"THAT girl, in the shop, I can't remember her name…, the one with the big hair…, a ghattis…, big bosom…, that's it, yes, Elaine, Elaine Jacobs, what a memory I've got, hey? That girl Elaine, I used to give her a tup. She thought she could blackmail me because I gave her a tup. She came to me. She wanted three bags of whitewash. I said, 'Sure', and I made out an invoice, 75 cents. So, she didn't pay for it. She thought because I gave her a tup, she wouldn't have to pay. So, I gave her over to the lawyer. 75 cents! She thought because I gave her a tup, she didn't have to pay. I gave her over to the lawyer. That tup wasn't worth 35 cents, never mind 75!"

…❧…

THE most potent image that remained of the sexuality of his youth was a dark black-and-white photograph of an eighteen-year-old at a youth camp.

The image shows a small crowd of youths gathered at the edge of a dam or lake. Two youths have grabbed him. He is bare-footed, wearing only long underwear, 'gatke's' as he called them, a one piece, long-sleeved, long-legged cream-colored underwear garment with a placket, 3 buttons at the neck, and elasticized cuffs at the wrist and ankle cuffs. One youth is holding his ankles, the other is holding his wrists. They appear as if they have swung him back and forth in an ever-increasing arc. The photograph shows the moment of the highest point of the forward movement of the arc, just prior to them letting go and dumping him in the river. He has a distinctly broad smile reflected on the faces of several of the other youths gathered around.

For many years this image held a potently mysterious fascination, a submerged potentiality for Shaye.

Similarly, a photograph of a white lynch mob gathered around the charred remains of a black man wrongfully accused of raping a white woman in Coatesville, Pennsylvania in 1914.

And again at that moment as the Master hung between the young Russian nurse and the swarthy Iranian aide in the hospital after the emergency operation to insert the stent that saved his life.

The daughter of his Dutch girlfriend yelled at the hospital admissions staff when she saw the Master collapsed in the chair in the Emergency room where he had been waiting for over an hour.

They immediately wheeled the Master into emergency surgery while the Dutch girlfriend called Shaye, who took the first flight out of the U.S.A.

. . . ❧ . . .

IN recovery, the Master complained of constipation amongst other symptoms, but he enjoyed the attentions of his cousins, his son, his attentive girlfriend, and the young, recently immigrated Russian nurse.

The nurse dutifully administered an enema in the privacy of the curtains drawn temporarily about the bed to seclude the procedure. In the common ward, various large families of varied extraction gathered around their loved ones, eating lunch, balancing the various condiments and foil wrapped delicacies about and on top of the bodies of the bedridden patients, mixing the heavy odor of cardamom, za'atar and garlic with the acrid pungency of antiseptics and salves.

Having completed inserting the enema and drawing back the curtains, the nurse informed the Master in her newly learned broken language that when the enema took effect, they would take him to the bathroom down the hall.

This didn't take very long and soon the pretty Russian nurse and the hairy Iranian male aide, encouraged and instructed by many of the visitors gathered at the bedsides, lifted his dead weight and carried him a few steps off the hospital bed, all the while talking to each other and to the Master in the melange of accented and incorrect gender nouns and misplaced adjectives that all three new immigrants used to communicate with each other.

As the Master hung, in that familiar position once again, the front of his hospital gown drawn taut between the nurse and the aide, open, loose and dragging its ties on the floor at the rear, revealing his transparent white and boney behind in the perfect V that his body formed below the canopy above him, somehow, the Master, misunderstood, misinterpreted, mistranslated, the instructions of the nurse and aide amid the cacophony of the ward.

Some instruction, fantasized, involuntary, intentionally or otherwise, told him to let go, at which point he dumped his entire bowel into a large pile on the floor.

So effective was the enema that the solids left his body at such a fast rate, volume and solidity, that the matter quickly formed a neat pyramid below him that almost touched his behind.

The daughter of his Dutch girlfriend, the Dutch girlfriend herself, Shaye, the pretty Russian nurse, the swarthy, hairy Iranian aide, the crowds of visitors, stared aghast in the now completely silent ward.

The Master simply hung there without comment, looking at the ceiling, expressionless, just as he did some years later at the airport in Orlando, Florida.

"Habima!".

...~...

Chapter 5

The Vial

THE Madam, smelling only slightly of the residues of pink Oil of Olay, had left him. The Master entertained himself with his girlfriend, the Lady from Iran, who lived downstairs from his apartment and who had 'entertained' him regularly over the years while his wife was at work. He paid for trips for her to Hong Kong and England, and several trips to the USA. She dumped him when two things occurred.

He became especially abusive to her granddaughter, whom she loved and dearly protected in the face of his repeated attempts to victimize the granddaughter with comments like "she's just using you to do nothing, just sits at home and talks to boys."

The Lady from Iran endured this victimization for some time, balancing his benefits to her against his deficits, until the balance weighed heavily to one side when the Lady from Africa knocked at the door.

The Master had taken a trip alone back to Africa where, amongst other visits, he visited his brother Issac's son, a successful business executive.

After several of the Master's uncomfortable encounters with the nephew's female office staff and their complaints to him, the nephew made sure the Master didn't come to his place of business any longer.

Instead, the nephew set him up on a date with a relative of his wife's.

After several dates and perhaps trysts with this woman, the Master returned home, leaving behind an open invitation to the woman to come and join him, which she did a couple of months later.

Only the Master had failed to inform his current girlfriend, the Iranian lady from downstairs, of the impending arrival or existence of the Lady from Africa.

The Master hadn't informed the Lady from Africa about the Lady from Iran, just like he told no one that his wife had left him, but let people know in his usual obtuse way of implied or inferred conclusions, that she was an incapacitated individual that he, in his generosity of spirit and understanding and obvious sacrifice in the face of loneliness, had sent back to Africa "where she will be taken better care of," he said.

Once the Lady from Africa became aware of the Lady from Iran, she left on the next available flight.

"This other woman, what does he think I am, a whore?", said the Iranian Lady to Shaye as they sat in her lounge surrounded by graphic prints by Cecil Skotnes, whom her now deceased Hungarian husband had represented at some point.

"Does he think I lie in his bed for this? No!"

For the duration of Shaye's visit, the Master continued to give the impression that he was still in a relationship with the Iranian Lady from downstairs.

They were all guilty of the deception. The Master invited the Iranian lady up for dinner and several visits, and Shaye and his partner endured and took part in the continuing deception, never letting on that they knew the truth of the circumstances.

Similarly with the implications of the Master 'visiting' the Iranian lady downstairs while his wife upstairs lay in the cold bathwater before she left him.

The terror this man wielded was extraordinary.

…☙…

THE resonance of these moments, the Master stretched between the youths, smiling, the lynch mob observing the burnt body before them as the flash of the camera ignites, the Master hanging between the Russian and the Iranian nurses above the mound of excrement on the polished floor, the TSA agent at the airport in Florida, these images echoed across the years where their correlation collided and merged into coincidental sharp focus.

There they existed in the indeterminable soup of confusion where they meet and merge with the image of a young child thrown into a swimming pool wrapped in a thick blanket.

…☙…

THE Master often sent parcels to his children. Mostly objects he had found in the street or that he had absconded from the collection boxes for refugees.

None-the-less these were gestures of contact with no particular agenda besides implying that he had purchased many of the items for the intended recipients, which he hadn't.

He also occasionally included articles on tax relief from the large print edition of the Reader's Digest, in addition to several prejudicial jokes.

…☙…

At first, the jokes he sent to Shaye were racist or right-wing views of politics, but as the years progressed, they focused on the mechanisms and onset of old age. As it did so, with time, the content increasingly centered on references to sexuality.

He had become a regular correspondent with a man in Southern California. Together they traded stamps back and forth until each, on the instigation of the other, included sexually explicit jokes in their letters. As their intimacy grew, so the Southern California man included pornographic images in his correspondence.

The images he included were from various mail order video catalogues. Page after page of miniature scenarios of couples and vaginas, column after column of stamp sized groups and various races of women dressed in leather or in nurses' uniforms gagging from extraordinarily large penises of men, boys or animals stuffed deep down their throats.

Month after month, the man from Southern California included these pages in his correspondence until eventually he and the Master established a regular correspondence that included detailed descriptions of both their ongoing personal sex lives, imagined, or enhanced, or otherwise. The Master mailed these gems of solitude to Shaye.

At first, including these pornographic images in the mail surprised Shaye, but he passed them off as his father's attempt at shared intimacy, perhaps even an obtuse reference to his son, finally gaining maturity in his father's eyes.

After all, on one occasion the Master decided to share his first sexual experience with Shaye.

When the Master included the actual correspondence and the printed catalogue materials from the man from Southern California, it became clear who was the source of the recent influx of pornography that arrived packaged together with plastic cocktail mixing sticks, a letter opener, or two, a pair of gloves, a battery, a twisted spoon or a sweater with a button missing.

Shaye tried in vain to have the Master discontinue his correspondence with this man from Southern California.

Shaye had recently become intrigued by the writings, rituals and modus operandi of serial killers and sexual predators, particularly the analysis by certain FBI profilers.

He also became intrigued by a series of informal photographs of murder scenes taken by police photographers in New York and California. It convinced him the man from Southern California either was or had been a sexual predator or serial killer, or at the very least, had all the makings of one.

Shaye conveyed his intuition to the Master, but the Master ignored the warnings and continued his correspondence with the man from California.

On one occasion, a parcel that arrived for the Master from the man from Southern California included a small glass vial of off-white semi-transparent fluid, epitomizing the climax of this correspondence. The accompanying letter described in great detail how the Master should insert the vial of semen into the vagina of the Master's current partner, the lady from Iraq.

The Master forwarded this parcel to Shaye.

The parcel he sent Shaye didn’t include the small glass vial of semen.

Chapter 6

The Airport (1)

THE Master, his Dutch girlfriend and Shaye, with his partner, took a trip to Disney World at the Master's request. This time, they actually reached the desired location.

The last time the Master traveled with Shaye, the Master had insisted he wanted to visit Mauritius. Shaye dutifully informed the Uncle in charge of the Master's funds in Africa, to purchase tickets from the Master's funds for a week's vacation to this tropical paradise.

On arrival at the airport in Mauritius, the Master exclaimed, "This isn't Madagascar!".

"No, it isn't. This is Mauritius. It's close to Madagascar, but it's not Madagascar," replied Shaye.

“Damn”, replied the Master, “I meant Madagascar. I always wanted to go to Madagascar.”

But he took advantage of the situation and helped himself to huge portions of food from the 24-hour buffet provided by this resort that could have been in any of many tropical locations so generic were its features and so disconnected was it from its surrounding culture.

On one trip to the dinner buffet, the Master and Shaye traversed the luminous azure swimming pools. It was night and the tropical sky blazed with the jewels of the galaxies unfettered by the glaze of pollution. Their light reflected on the rippling water and the goggles of several children snorkeling in the winding pools. There were several pools with connecting concrete bridges not over 2-foot-wide traversing and connecting each pool to the other and finally to the cabana with the displays of food.

Children swam between the pools, diving momentarily beneath the footpaths and reappearing in the next pool. Like seals, they played with each other in devilish games of chase, accompanied by exclamations of joy in various dialects of Swedish and Italian.

The Master stopped suddenly midway on one of these bridges. Shaye almost collided with him, only barely maintaining his balance by grabbing onto the Master’s shoulder to prevent himself from falling into the water

The Master was unperturbed. He stood there, unbuckled his belt, pulled down his zipper, extricated his penis, urinated at length into the pool, pulled up his zipper, buckled his belt, and proceeded to the buffet cabana saying, “Let's eat!”.

He ate voluminously, without hesitation, and with multiple trips to the buffet. Just as he did years later at Disney world.

…❧…

SHAYE had spent weeks planning this trip for the Master at the Master’s request, as he had for all the trips the Master made in the past 10 years.

For days Shaye shuttled the Master and his girlfriend, the Dutch Lady. Shaye dutifully constructed a ramp for the hired van and loaded two rental scooters into and out of the van at each tourist stop along the way, walking behind the couple as they zoomed around.

Shaye kept embarrassingly silent as the Master grabbed at the Dutch Lady in the van's rear and she giggled and squealed in feigned delight and unavailability.

Shaye and his partner, not really wanting to visit Disney world or Florida for the umpteenth time, dutifully accompanied the Master in this splurge of grandiose generosity towards the Dutch Lady. They both had to give up their vacations, pay for the dog care, find and hire substitutes who could take care of the business in case of emergencies.

As a slight gesture towards his partner's efforts and patience, on the return journey to the airport, Shaye stopped off at a highly recommended Cuban restaurant close to the airport.

The day before, the Master had purchased a large quantity of Pringles potato chips at the discount club store, not the quantity one purchases at the convenience store, or the grocery store or the supermarket. These were the Super Jumbo Maxi Barely Wrap Your Arms Around size. The size that usually only appears to some in dreams.

Unbeknownst to anyone and given the enormous quantities of MSG added to the Pringles, the Master had already eaten large quantities of these chips in secrecy at the hotel that morning. Not just a lot, not just many, a large quantity, a Super Jumbo Maxi quantity.

Perhaps this was solace for falling asleep for the entire Cirque du Soleil extravaganza the night before. He had done something similar when he had insisted on going to bed early instead of joining the others for a joyous celebration of old Rumanian Jewish tenderloin and gribenes dinner on the Lower East side in New York City and then attempted to make everyone feel guilty at his exclusion and then having a good time without him.

His solace was to steal one crystal from a lamp in the Waldorf-Astoria Hotel, which he later had made into a necklace for the Dutch lady.

He also refused to believe Shaye had found a great deal on-line for the Waldorf, despite Shaye sending him the invoices. Instead, he decided, with typical splitting and triangulation, to report to Rebecca that Shaye was indulging himself at his expense. His anger at not being at the Rumanian dinner found justice in that aside, communicated in what should have been a whisper but wasn't.

There were so many such coincidences in his life.

A similar chandelier crystal lay for years on the shelf in the bar in his house with the fake ship's prow, right next to the book of matches from Jack Dempsey's New York restaurant and the small copper Eiffel Tower. That crystal he claimed he had found on the floor of the Vatican in Rome.

Now they stood in the TSA security line at the airport in Orlando, Florida.

…❧…

Chapter 7

The Airport (2)

THE Master and his Dutch girlfriend regularly used the ruse they called "Habima".

What is the ruse called 'Habima' one may ask?

Habima was the name of the world-renowned theater in Tel-Aviv. The two of them adopted this name as the means to communicate their specific intentions when amongst strangers to each other.

The ruse was used to falsely present themselves as being blind, or hard of hearing, or unable to walk.

The ruse was the means to get better seats on an aircraft, to request mini liquor bottles as frequently as possible during the flight, get extra meals, and wheeled through security and onto the aircraft ahead of the other passengers.

The ruse was essentially based on an inner need to 'get one over', to fool others to your undeserved benefit.

To fool others, as the Master did with the Glenlivet, as he'd done with his false tale of his sister's death, as he did to validate his accusation that Shaye had stolen his money.

To ostensibly lie as he so often did.

To lie, to cover his emptiness, his unimportance, his vanity, his cruelty, his violence, his survival.

…❧…

THE Master and his mistress lined up waiting in the TSA security line at the Orlando Airport in Florida. The Master, having called 'Habima' to the mistress as they exited the rental vehicle, were both now comfortably ensconced in wheelchairs pushed by airport staff.

A large African American female TSA agent resplendent in a large long blonde curly haired wig, beckons the Master, walking stick between his knees forward to the metal detector arch.

The Master wheeled himself the scant couple of feet to the entrance of the metal detector arch.

"No, no, no. You can't go through the metal detector with a wheelchair. Get up. Can you walk?" said the TSA agent.

"Get up. You can't go through in a wheelchair. It's regulations, get up," said the TSA agent.

The Master sat slumped in the wheelchair, silently looking forward and making no effort to cooperate.

"Here, I'll help you get up. Take my hands, I will support you, but first you must put your metallic things in this basket," says the TSA agent.

"Habima!" the Master mutters to his mistress, a slight smirk appearing undisguised on his face.

The TSA agent holds out the woven plastic basket for the Master as she takes his one hand and pulls him forward out of the wheelchair.

To appear cooperative, the Master, stiff legged and frozen in his seated posture, allows the TSA agent to lift him from the wheelchair and forward towards the metal detector arch.

As she drew him forward, he proceeded to projectile vomit over the front of the ample bosom of the TSA agent, into the plastic woven basket, and all over the floor of the metal detector arch.

The basket, still held by the TSA agent, dripped with heavy and bright orange Pringles particulate mixed with the spicy Cuban food he had scoffed down at the restaurant barely a half hour before.

Shaye, his partner and the Dutch mistress, stood there aghast.

The Master, stood there silently immobile with vomit splattered shoes.

...❧...

Chapter 8

Two Hundred and Fifty Dollars

MRS. T: "I feel so sorry for him. I mean, you don't know who to trust anymore. I mean, he told me how they caught the person who stole his money. He said they fired her on the spot! Gave a fabulous speech last night, your father, just fabulous."

Shaye: "Oh I didn't know he had money stolen."

Mrs. T: "Oh yes, a lot of money. He had it in his room just before a trip overseas with Jane. He said they caught her, the one that took the money. You know they all have a master key. They caught her, fired her on the spot! Shame for the poor man, can't blame him, you know. People take advantage, you know."

. . . ~ . . .

Dutch Lady: "Yes, it happened. We were going on a trip to America. He kept his money at my house. He didn't want it at the home because he said someone had been taking money from there, from the rooms. He said they caught that person. It was one maid that's cleaning. Anyway, so I brought him two hundred and fifty dollars, two hundreds and I think twenties, and a ten. I'm not sure about the twenties. His money, from my house."

Shaye: "Ok, so what happened then?"

Dutch Lady: "So some time later, some days, a week, something, I was putting away one of his shirts in his room, and there in the pocket was the money. All of it. So, I give it to him and I say, "You have to go to tell you found it. This person, the aide, was accused. You have to go tell!"

Shaye: "And you're sure it was the same money, the money you brought from your place?"

Dutch Lady: "Yes, just like it was before, two hundreds and twenties. I'm not so sure about the twenties but two hundreds for sure, yes."

. . . ~ . . .

SHAYE: "So, what happened with this stolen money?"

Social Worker: "Ah yes, it happened. He was making a trip, and he had this money in the apartment. He came to me very upset, telling me that his money is gone. Very upset, really. He was shaking all over. So, then some days later he came to me in the office, furious, shouting, very furious. He said he had found the money in his locker, in an envelope, the exact amount."

Shaye: "Really!'

Social Worker: "Yes, he knew it was not his money because it was in different notes. Someone had taken the money, and later put it back in his locker, but not the same money. Two hundred and fifty dollars, yes, but not the same money."

Shaye: "How did he know it was different money? Did he have serial numbers written? Did he remember all the denominations?"

Social Worker: "Yes, yes. He said that his money was two hundred and fifty dollars. Two one hundred and one fifty-dollar note."

Shaye: "Did you see the money from the locker?"

Social Worker: "Yes, yes. He showed me the envelope from his locker. A lot of small bills, no hundred-dollar bills."

Shaye: "I don't know, this sounds a little strange. Did this really happen? I don't know why, but something doesn't sound right. You know he invents a lot of stuff."

Social Worker: "I know, but I saw him, really he was shaking, really, so upset, furious, shouting."

Shaye: "Ah yes, he is an excellent actor."

Social Worker: "Ah yes, he is acting often."

...❧...

MASTER: "So why are you speaking to the social worker and the others?"

Shaye: "Well, they wanted me to know that they had tried to take care and clean the apartment, but you got angry. They didn't want me to think that they hadn't tried to take care."

Master: "Yes, of course I got angry. I told them. I told them in no uncertain terms. I laid down the law. Nobody in my apartment! Nobody! They stole my money! I told Lynn (the Director of the facility), nobody in my apartment and I wrote it in a letter, not even you Lynn! That's it. And what did they do? I was away in hospital, and they had three, the head woman and two others, and they came in and ..."

Shaye: "But Daddy, they were trying to help you. They wanted to take care. They didn't have bad intentions."

Master: "They did what they wanted, not what I wanted!"

Shaye: "Well, is that so bad? They had no ill intent. They weren't trying to hurt you."

Master: "Yes, it's bad. (now shouting loudly) I'm not a piece of meat! I still have a head! I still have a memory! Last night I gave a speech. All the ladies in the corridor say how wonderful it was. I told them, not in my room! Not without my permission! And they didn't do it! I am the tenant! I have rights! I pay! They stole my money! They hired a plainclothes detective, and he stayed around, watching, and they caught her, he caught her. I was going to take a trip to America, to Florida, to you, to your sister. Two hundred and fifty dollars I had and gone! I told them, never! I told them, never in my room, not even Lynn! (shouting louder) I'm not a piece of meat! I can still think! I can still do!"

Shaye: "But Daddy, they were trying to help…"

Master: "Only in their way, how they want, not how I want! Not how I want!"

Shaye: "And what way is that?"

Master: "Stay out of my room! They stole my money!"

…❧…

MASTER: "Goodbye my boy, goodbye."

Shaye, on entering the taxi to the airport: "Goodbye Daddy."

Master: "Ay, ay, ay. My son, don't let it end this way."

Shaye: "What way? What do you mean?"

Master: (No answer.)

Shaye: "I am still your son. You are still my father. Nothing will change that."

…❧…

Everything that happens will happen today,
nothing has changed, but nothing's the same,
and ev'ry tomorrow could be yesterday,
and everything that happens will happen today,

- David Byrne and Brian Eno
'Everything That Happens wiil Happen Today'

Chapter 9

The Ultimate Vanity

THE Master had reached a point in his life that many confront. That point where your volition is reversed. That point where you understand that your place in the whole is minimal. Perhaps it even means nothing more than you were here and soon you will be gone. As will the already fading memory of who you were, or what you did, perhaps good, perhaps bad, no matter what you bequeathed to whom, or why, or how much retribution one might try to wreak from the grave, it will all be gone soon, and forever.

Yet blinded by obsession with pursuing importance, obstinately obsessed with the determination for relevance and the desperate need for cowering victims, he doggedly waded through the mire of soggy chaff and attempted in a variety of ways to plan a profile of consequence for himself in his old age without the Madam.

He hired a middle-aged Russian recent immigrant to push him around in his wheelchair and whom he constantly tried to portray to others as his 'girlfriend'. The Other, how you are perceived by others, is the most important. Always.

Finally, in a desperate gesture towards sanctity, towards memory in the infinity of the forgotten, he committed the ultimate indulgence of supreme vanity.

In that cause, he had often tainted his children in one form or another.

But now, in his old age, and given a propensity towards violence and victimization, in a gesture of defiance against the odds, against the tide of time, against the volume of lies and falsities, he finally sacrificed his youngest son, Shaye at the altar.

Not unlike the Abraham of his forefathers, he agreed to the bitterness of his oldest daughter, Rebecca, in her guilty pursuit of Shaye. She accused her brother of theft of the Master's money, of elder abuse. She threatened him with criminal charges and court proceedings. She vilified him to her family, to cousins, to nephews, to distant uncles and aunts.

Yet the Master sat silent, knowing full well the emptiness of her accusations against her brother, his son, that she accused on his behalf, wholly unaware of his mechanical desperation for the pandering attentions of others he so craved, in fact couldn't survive without, waiting for the judgment of death to lift him from this quagmire of deception and deceit of his own creation, leaving his victims to struggle to the surface if they could.

...❧...

THE Master spent over twenty minutes of non-stop screaming at the Shaye. This was the third time Shaye had called that week. Each time, the Master followed the same approach. Screaming unintelligibly nonstop for lengthy periods punctuated by "where's my money!" repeatedly.

Master: "Huh...? What…? I can't hear you…"

Shaye: "I said, is that all you are interested in? Is that all you want? Money? If that's all you want, you have a decision to make. Do you want a son or do you want money?"

Master: "Huh…? What…? I can't hear, what?"

Shaye: "Do... you… want… a… son… or… do… you... want… money?"

Master: "What…? I can't… what ...?"

Shaye: "Oh, you can hear what I said perfectly."

Master: "Are you calling me a liar?!"

…❧…

THE Master was not known for his subtlety of thought, especially while in the throes of a hysterical outburst. Nor was he adept at asking questions, without malice or foregone conclusion.

The Master, like his surrogate daughter, could not imagine or articulate an understanding of what Shaye was asking him. Their bitterness and inexorable desire for revenge suffocated in their self-fulfilling presumptuousness.

If the Master answered *'Money',* he was negating 60 years of a relationship with Shaye and reveal once again his penchant for laying the traps of victimization.

If the Master answered *'Son',* for Shaye there would have been no question. The Master would have whatever money he needed or wanted.

Shaye's view of the relationship with the Master was not transactional in the same way the masters view was.

In the vortex that led to this emotional attack on him, Shaye had gone so far as to promise the Master on many occasion that he would care for him no matter the circumstance financially or otherwise, even if it meant repaying money the Master had given as a gift or as a loan with no due date or means of redemption.

If that circumstance came about would he ask Rebecca to repay the tens of thousands of dollars he had given or loaned her all the years?

Would he demand Nathan pay back the money he had provided to purchase two apartments, which Nathan sold, did not return any of the money but asked for money for a third apartment?

The Master had often made it clear to Shaye that Rebecca and Nathan were to receive nothing by inheritance. He also made sure to make it clear that Shaye's inheritance would be, at least, in part, the 'loans' he had made to him already.

"Your sister doesn't need to know. The grandchildren, yes, but not for her. She said the stuff I sent her was junk! She got rid of all my mementos, my trophies for winning at bowls, my medals, my plaques in honor, she got rid of them to you. She said, "I want nothing to do with him!" Me, yes me, she wants nothing to do with me! But the money she'll take!"

"And London", as he called Nathan, "can go to hell."

Many years before, the Master, for reasons unclear to Shaye, had taken him to the US bank where he held his funds. Saying to Shaye, "Rebecca has been helping herself to the account without asking. I'm going to take her name off. You will have signature."

With that simple but undiscussed deliberation, with the transfer of those funds, Shaye became the Master's de facto accountant, trustee, vacation reservation agent, surrogate gift maker to the grandchildren, international money transferee on behalf of cousins, and much more.

Shaye was quite taken aback at this sudden delegation of responsibility. The Master had never trusted him with something as important, as vulnerable as this, except the several occasions he had left him, age seventeen, to look after the store while he and the Madam vacationed for months in Europe and the Americas.

Shaye took on the task of managing his funds determined to meet the responsibility in the dull conciseness of the ordained, as a duty of son to father.

Until, many years later, suddenly the Master told Shaye to transfer the majority of the funds back to his sole signature in the 'Holy Land'. Shaye obediently did so without question or consideration for the reasoning behind the transfer.

Until, shortly thereafter, the Master told Shaye he wanted to leave $10,000 to each of Rebeccas Grandchildren in his will. To which Shaye replied, "It's your money, you do what you want."

...~...

UNTIL the Master neared his death and his first and only encounter with the terror of existential anguish.

The ruse of his '*Habimah*' eventually couldn't be contained amidst the flood of rejection he had endured these past years. That reservoir of hate, that dam of disappointment and frustration found its outlet at the gates of self-manufactured crisis, flooding, suffocating, and eventually pushing inexorably towards suicide, that object that he had always held so conveniently close to himself, for himself, Shaye.

He suddenly ranted on the phone to Shaye for hours uninterrupted.

Suddenly Shaye had stolen his money.

Suddenly he wanted Shaye to provide check by cheque accounting of the past 20 years despite Shaye always providing these to him through the years.

When Shaye refused to make the effort to audit the accounts, Shaye suggested they should hire an independent accountant.

"That will be too expensive!" was the reply.

He was determined to wreak revenge on Shaye from omitting his name from the Madam's tombstone.

The Master cried, he howled. In impotent spite he promised to live forever!

His lawyer said aghast, "I have never seen such pain in my life!"

The flotsam and jetsam of an inarticulate man with the ultimate subliminal realization of oncoming defeat at the hands of his life and the finality of his motivations of spite and revenge.

…❧…

THE task of the son is to do better than the father.

The father and the son both see that.

The father encourages the son to achieve that goal.

The son recognizes the task is his duty.

But there is a condition.
The son shouldn't do that much better that he humiliates the father.

…❧…

THERE simply is no greater vanity than to sacrifice ones own in the service of self grandeur.
Was this Abraham at the altar, knife drawn, willing to slit the throat of his son?
Did he plan to stab him fatally in the heart?
Did he bind the son with rope?
Did he blindfold him?
Did the son struggle, or resist?
Was the son unconscious, struck from behind with a rock, or a heavy stick?
Or did he lie there willingly, convinced by his father's ruse?
There simply is no greater vanity than to sacrifice ones own in the service of self grandeur.

…❧…

Shaye balancing on one foot

REBECCA jumped at the opportunity to savage Shaye in her efforts to assuage her guilt for abandoning her father all those years in favor of her in-laws and the almighty dollar.

Her fervor was fueled by her inexorable volition to curry favor with the Other, that impression that others will have of her, speculative as that might be.

Her pose as the dedicated daughter defending her father lay in the shadow of her blatant disregard for her mother who was so needy, and critical, and self-effacing and herself resigned to her daughter's facets of vengeance so very similar to those her husband had foisted on her so many times.

. . . ❧ . . .

Chapter 10

Lying

AT first it appeared as simply 'fibbing'.

There was no more chocolate.

At times, it appeared as deceit.

He sought to justify his prodding and grabbing at the breasts of the secretary.

At times, it appeared to be subterfuge.

He replaced the Glenlivet whisky with the cheaper brand and watched and listened as his guests were fooled and fooled themselves as they complimented him on the superior taste of the Glenlivet, as he too was fooled by the tea added to the 'Glenlivet' by Lilian.

At other times, it appeared to be legitimate.

Simply by not saying anything in reply, he accepted the presumptions of others. By omission, he accepted the compliments for making the chips that Ettie made.

To the child, it began with the story of his adventures in the second world war.

His scar from having his appendix removed became "the bayonet that the German soldier stuck in my stomach."

The ultimate lies were the lies he believed himself. These were lies where the lie is the truth, the truth is a lie, and he had 'forgotten' that he had lied, when he preferred to accept the lie as more advantageous than the truth and now the lie is all he knew and he believed it to be the truth even though it was a lie.

What started out as an effort to elevate his status or convince someone of something, or defend himself against something, or someone, became himself.

The ultimate deceit, self-deceit.

...❧...

Chapter 11

Silence

THE Master died today.

It surprisingly didn't make the day any different for Shaye. There was no sense of relief or sadness, no regret or sympathy. Nothing suddenly rose out of the background, drowning the noise of daily rituals, consuming oneself with convulsing sobs of mourning.

No, there wasn't even a sense of numbness, the neutrality of defenses against those feelings that might betray the hurt or the anger.

Even the thought of him wrapped in a shroud on a bed, or laying in a box in the ground somewhere, eyes now shut after the final terror, didn't bring any thoughts of thankfulness for the termination of his pain nor nostalgia for some past warmth or conviviality. Even the faint glimmer of insight into the trajectory of another's' life, as is so often the case when faced with their death, never appeared.

No, it was rather simply the faint echo, a vague memory of someone one knew some time ago in some other place, some other time, some vague familiarity of detail that has outlines but no weight. He had worked so hard to eliminate the bonds, the trust, the respect of a lifetime, gone in the anger of his fading final years, aided so adeptly by his daughter. There was very little left to mourn over when he finally physically left. For Shaye, he had died a thousand times over the past 3 years since they had last spoken.

Rebecca announced his death to her friends and family in a message that revealed not only her naivete but her particular penchant for theatrical exaggeration in the pursuit of the creation of illusion she had so clearly inherited from her father.

She wrote: "My father and your long-lost cousin passed away peacefully in Israel. Just how he wanted to. His lifelong dream to be part of the land of Israel was realized."

In actuality, the Master hated Israel. He hated Israelis, he particularly hated Israeli children.

Rebecca had taken it upon herself to arrange his burial and to erect his tombstone immediately rather than return a year later, as custom provides. It was just so much cheaper to do both at the same time.

This was only her second visit in 30 years and she was as fearful of terrorist attacks as she always had been, so much so when her father was barely recovering from multiple surgeries some years before, instead of visiting him, she took a trip to Italy where she met Nathan and enjoyed an amicable vacation on the Riviera.

...⁂...

Chapter 12

There are no Innocent Victims (1)

IT had taken a bit of investigating to find the cemetery where he was buried, but not very long to find the place of his grave. It seemed Rebecca had made a point of not allowing Shaye to know why, when, or where he had died or buried. Instead, she chose to inform Shaye's lawyer of his passing.

"Please inform Shaye that his father has died."

No date, no cause, no place, no burial location.

Simply, "Please inform Shaye that his father has died."

Was this her ultimate gesture of power, another jab between the ribs? Was this communication part of her overwhelming desire for revenge, just like her father would have done?

Revenge for what?

Was this yet another gesture toward her guilt at inheriting everything?

Was this an extraordinary lack of empathy towards the humanity of others?

Only she would know.

What more of a sign of her lack of understanding of the familial entanglements that both she and both her brothers had endured, how the children were consumed by their parents' need to triangulate, to pit one sibling against the other, each their own distorted character of the parents, each to their own ends.

It was surprising to find the spot and how unremarkable in every way it was. There was no residue of the ceremony that might or might not have taken place over his dead and silent body. The mumbled prayers, the remarks, the gestures, the glances, all gone now, or never existed to begin with.

The hollow grandiosity of his vanity and obsession with the Other wasn't visible at all. The bile of his anger and viciousness didn't boil up to saturate the surrounding ground in rivulets through the dirt, soaking those unknowns innocently buried around him. His burial mound was simply silent, touched only by the heat of the blazing sun so bright in its intensity it almost eliminated any detail.

It was almost midday. Children hadn't finished the school day. In the distance, one could hear them singing in a classroom, an old song filled with dreams of socialism, of a new vibrant life, of the juices and taste of the fruits of spring.

The heat of the desert has a peculiar way of transmitting certain sounds over long distances, the sound of electricity in transformers, the sounds of young joy, the chop chop chop of helicopter blades as they patrol the shoreline, the clatter of dishes being washed, the evening news on television. The blinding, stinging sand of the Hamsin blowing in from Saudi Arabia only momentarily mutes the sounds that become especially clear and vibrant in the pregnant silence before the sandstorm hits.

The burial spot reflected none of this. It lay mute, incapable of response, static as if stricken by the same shock of realization that rendered its incapacity. The same shock of confrontation, of resilience, the same struggle of defiant rage against submission to the power of that other Other. The other Other of the inevitable castration, the other Other that peers through the shrouds of deception, the other Other that is nothing, that is nothing but a mirror of contemptuous delight in seeing the Master struggle against the overwhelming tide of his frail indulgence, where he finally becomes his own victim, not able to draw his last breath, caught in the vicious struggle against himself, etched into the silent scream that rigor mortis did not need to enshrine, it's job already done. Death was no relief for him, it was simply suffocation at the hands of his own body, spluttering asphyxiation from the lack of oxygen, the aneurysm as it strikes the brain, or the heart as the stent fails.

The wave of silence struck again. The hopes of redemption, the hopes of acceptance, the hopes for an apology were over. There was nothing left. He left behind nothing in his will but the means to allow his daughter to feed on his perversity and her own, for a time, for a short time, and then that too would be gone.

The families at some of the surrounding graves seemed oblivious to my presence. They stood as I did, some looking at the sky, some heads bent, muttering a prayer. There were few in the cemetery alone as I was. Most stood in groups, especially those that seemed to have gathered at what was an obviously fresh grave.

At the far end of the cemetery, a figure in a group suddenly leaned on the person next to her before falling to the ground where she lay unmoving but sobbing until two others raised her gently and stood at her side as their ceremony continued.

"Yisgadal v-yiskadash ...."

...❧...

Chapter 13

There are no Innocent Victims (2)

THE rush, the vortex of contained responses, was overwhelming. All these past few years of not responding, not taking the bait, enduring the belittling attempts to victimize me by him and his surrogates, my sister, the lawyers, the regret, the court case, the litigation, the financial pressure, the emotional disease.

Out of the past, out of the future, into the present, there was no distinction between them now.

The veil of the past moved to the side, revealing a Sunday morning. Rebecca was barely a teenager. She was named after her father's mother, and he always remarked how she looked so similar to her.

Rebecca had gone out the night before, to a party, perhaps a Bat mitzvah or a Bar Mitzvah. Like most teenagers, she always wanted to sleep late on a

Sunday morning. This Sunday morning, she slept late, oblivious to the sound of the newspaper placed gently at the back door, to the battle for the comics page and those of Prince Valiant.

The Master edged the door open just slightly, peering into the quiet of the half-light only slightly pierced by the slash of light from the open door that ran across the floor, over the bed, her legs, the bed again, and up the opposite wall, ending in an abrupt sharp sliver.

He opened the door wider now, revealing his daughter wholly as she lay sleeping in bed, her dark hair spread against the pillow, her breath gently falling, her mouth open, her neck only slightly revealed at the opening of the lace edged pajama-top from OK Bazaars.

Motioning to Nathan and Shaye, he pushed them towards the end of the bed, quietly lifting up Shaye, just six years old, and setting him silently and gently at the end of the bed as Nathan crawled up and over the end of the bedstead.

"Yes, yes, go on, do it now," the Master whispered hoarsely at the door, a big smile on his face, barely able to contain his excitement and joy.

The two boys then did as their father instructed them previously behind the closed door.

They stood on the end of the bed, pulled down their pajama pants, and pissed into the face and mouth of their sleeping sister.

. . . ❧ . . .

THE color was bright yellow and strangely clear in the sharp focus of the midday sun. The stream had at first an arc of trajectory that ran almost parallel to the ground, such was the force of release. As the stream hit the surface, it splattered violently, yet held a peculiar choreographic beauty as if held in slow motion, drops colliding into each other, separating, turning, twisting, elongating into ever smaller globules only to collide with one another to form a larger drop bursting with vitality or splitting into several smaller drops that raced to the ground.

There was no shame in what seemed such an absurd desire as the first hints of swelling cursed through his body. The desire was initially excused as perhaps the early onset of incontinence or the late recall of enuresis as a child or simply the variety of nature. The sudden acceptance of what the body knows, but the mind refuses to acknowledge until its urgency overwhelms all notions of courtesy or appropriateness, of convenience, respect or courtesy and simply manifests itself as the banshee that it is, in the form, at the time and place that it chooses.

Within that shroud of shrill and piercing silence he stood and pissed on his fathers grave, long and hard, as long as the pressure held, hard and loud until there was nothing more, hard and loud until there was no more dust on the letters that now glistened, no more fluid, no more need, no more want, no more desire for revenge, for acceptance, for retribution, for forgiveness, for resolution, for blessing, until there was silence again, until the last urine dripped down his pants leg and crept between his toes.

...❧...

NOW he understood the vortex of his family's shame and guilt, their defense against the obvious and the championing of the obscure and the unsaid, of that call for some kind of morality, of some answer to the undeniable weight of the inheritance of behaviors, the influence of the learned, the models of Good and Bad, of the Other, of the other Other, of that which is beyond our power to withstand, defeat or understand, the volition, the weight of the past.

They had all suffered, perhaps equally, perhaps not. It doesn't matter. They continued to seek, to find solace by convincing themelves and others of the justice of their cause, in the sanctity of their actions of retribution, in the appropriateness of their defiance, their defense and their attack, in the justice of their isolation.

The Great Cause, the notion of Family, Brother, Sister, Father, Mother, Kindness, Selflessness, Charity, the Good, were nothing but a fleeting illusion of naïve youth, of blind faith, of blind trust in the obtuse notion of family, of blind acceptance crushed in the face of perversity of astounding proportion and complexity.

...❧...

THE urine refused to be absorbed by the sand and stone. The rivulets spread over the ground, crept over the area in a web of glistening liquid until it gathered near the headstone in a pool which stood for a while reflecting what were now a few scattered clouds in the sky and the fleeting shadow of a high-flying bird.

Then, just as suddenly as it had formed and remained, the web disappeared into the sand, leaving nothing but a darker, slightly swollen patch that dried within minutes, leaving only a slight shiny trace at its edges, like that of a snail.

I've given up talking about God a long time ago. I, at the same time, continue to struggle to identify the presence of the Divine, moments in life which, given my theological and my cultural background, I perceive as the presence of God. And miraculously, that presence of God happens, I think, where relations begin to be restored.

I talk about my colleague Nyameka Goniwe, whose husband was Mathew Goniwe, one of the Cradock Four, who was killed by the security police.

We created a situation where she sat down with one of the security police who gave the order for her husband to be killed, and she said to him, "You know, Colonel, there is absolutely nothing you can give me. I don' want your money. You can't give me my husband back. All I'm looking for is a signal of your humanity, and if I see that, through acknowledgement, through humility, then I, as a vulnerable human being, am required to explore the possibility of being reconciled to you."

Interview by Krista Tippett, 'Speaking of Faith', National Public Radio, with Charles Villa-Vicencio, Executive Director, Institute for Justice and Reconciliation, Cape Town, South Africa, August 29, 2004

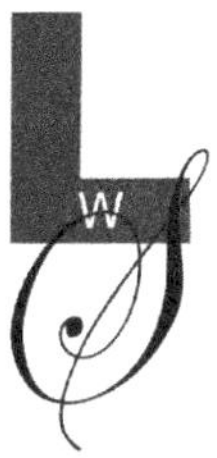
W

LIVING WITHOUT SHADOWS

Looking at the night sky knowing that I am seeing the past in the present, that there will be continuity, at least for a time. That there is some comfort in knowing the universe is expanding and not contracting, that the notions of Hegel or Heidegger, of Satre or Jung, of Einstein or Hawkins, are just that, notions and speculations, inferences or calculations, theories of perception or responsibility, or of the human condition in the face of all of this. That there is experience without attachment to buildings or love, experience with no sense of profit or loss, of gain or retreat, where that experience is not a possession, not a qualifier nor an asset. It just is.

CPSIA information can be obtained
at www.ICGtesting.com
Printed in the USA
LVHW071403241122
733912LV00021B/968